Praise for André Narbonne's *Twelve Miles to Midnight*:

"*Twelve Miles to Midnight* feels like so much more than the sum of its parts, never straying from the small particulars of ordinary lives yet somehow achieving the breadth and depth of an epic. Narbonne writes with a rare humanity and insight, giving all his characters their due and uniquely attuned to the ties that bind them."

—Nino Ricci, author of *The Origin of Species*

"Though *Twelve Miles to Midnight* covers lots of cold, hard territory—from Northern Ontario, to Cape Breton, to an ice-bound tanker trapped off the coast of Newfoundland—there is no denying the intimate warmth of Narbonne's writing, the careful craftsmanship of his stories, and the tenderness of his characterization. This is one beautiful, tough book, full of complex relationships and sometimes angry compassion. I bet David Adams Richards and Herman Melville could appreciate what's happening in here. I hope you will, too."

—Alexander MacLeod, author of *Light Lifting*

"These are stories of loss—lost jobs, lost loved ones, lost lives. People lost to cancer, accident, their own hand. Lost childhood and lost relationships. Their consolation is to tell the stories, the old hope that to set down the right words in the right order has the power not to make sense of loss but simply to remember it. *Twelve Miles to Midnight* is a superbly crafted gift: honest, compelling, and deeply moving."

—Nick Mount, University of Toronto

"Narbonne writes authentically and acutely..."

—Sarah Murdock, *Toronto Star*

A good short story is not to be rushed but savoured. These characters in transformation in *Twelve Miles to Midnight* are human and poignant, the stories so compelling that they stay with the reader long after the book is closed. For good reason, this collection was shortlisted for the Danuta Gleed Literary Award.

—Patricia Sandberg, *The Miramichi Reader*

"*Twelve Miles to Midnight* is straightforward, yet complex; unadorned, yet poetic; to the point, yet evocative. And always, there's an element of mystery, discovery…. These are finely-crafted stories—they're rarely more than 3000 words long—that contain the seeds of much more. Highly recommended."

—Lee Thompson, *Atlantic Books Today*

Praise for short stories:

"Abuzz with the intense passions and devastating self-doubt of adolescence…emerging love and parental rifts that engages with, above all, its sharp, humorous style."

—Stephanie Bolster for "Darren, Almost in Love"

"[A] lovely amalgam of Arctic mystery, shipboard claustrophobia and human misery…"

—Douglas Glover, *Best Canadian Stories 06* for "The Advancements"

"[A] cut-throat, pensive story that takes us from the desolate 1960's mining towns of Northern Ontario to the ramshackle streets of a bygone Halifax and onwards to the volatile, ice-bound coast of Labrador. It is beyond a doubt destined to find its place on the upper shelves of modern Canadian fiction."

—Joel Thomas Hynes, David Adams Richards Prize Judge

LUCIEN &OLIVIA

ANDRÉ NARBONNE

Black Moss Press

2022

For Tom

Whitehots   Nov. 8, 2022 $18.90

Library and Archives Canada Cataloguing in Publication

Title: Lucien and Olivia / a novel by André Narbonne.
Names: Narbonne, André, 1963- author.
Identifiers: Canadiana 20210380853 |
ISBN 9780887536328 (softcover)
Classification: LCC PS8627.A7 L83 2002 | DDC C813/.6—dc23

Typeset and design: Chris Andrechek

Published by Black Moss Press
2450 Byng Road
Windsor, ON N8W 3E8 Canada
www.blackmosspress.com

Black Moss books are distributed in Canada and the U.S. by Fitzhenry &
Whiteside. All orders should be directed there. Black Moss Press acknowledges
the support of the Canada Council for the Arts and the Ontario Arts Council
for its publishing program.

PRINTED IN CANADA

Contents

Prologue

SIX MONTHS LATER, a hook fell from the sky, a sixty-five pound, case-hardened, inverted question mark stamped with the manufacturer's name, Waters & Co. The four men below heard the snap of the cable, the protest of the winch jolting free. They looked up to see their latest disaster falling noiselessly, precisely. In an instant, three of the men leaped out of its path. The fourth waited on the implied question.

1. April–June

A man lives by the side of the tracks and every morning at the same time the same train predictably passes his house yet somehow manages to hit him. Discuss.
—Graffiti found in the men's bathroom in the Department of Philosophy at Dalhousie University around the time this story is set.

SMU JOCKS
SUCK MOOSE COCKS
—Written underneath.

AN UNSEASONABLY COOL St. Catharines night at the beginning of June 1982 and a ship's fourth engineer stands half-in a payphone on Lakeshore Road.

He holds in one hand a pink post-it, on it, in elegant script, the name Olivia and a phone number. The other hand is bloody—gripping a smashed receiver, the cord dangling loose. Across the street, dimly visible through a dense fog, a package freighter churning upbound from Lock One, pushes towards Lake Erie. The man at the booth slumps against the glass, oblivious to the throb and hum of the freighter, pressing the shattered plastic and exposed wires to his ear.

On the other side of Lakeshore, behind a gated fence with a sign that reads KEEP OUT, a bent and ancient line handler is of two minds about what he's just witnessed: a vandal smashing a telephone or an idiot trying to use it. He inventories the other man's features in case he's asked to testify.

Late-twenties/early thirties
5' 10"ish
clean-shaven

light brown hair
jean jacket
blue, buttoned shirt tucked into black jeans—no belt
white runners

A coughing fit he can't contain, explosive and dangerously intimate, reveals him to the man in the booth.

The engineer replaces the ruined receiver and crosses the road.

"Any other payphones nearby?"

The line handler rubs his chin. "Nope." Deep and hoarse, his voice says he's been smoking since grade school. A network of wrinkles snake from his forehead to his eyes, from his lips to his chin, the deep channels suggesting lines carved aggressively onto Halloween pumpkins.

The engineer opens the gate and enters. "No other payphones in the city?"

"Closest I can think of is Lakeshore Mall."

"How far?"

"Buddy, the mall's closed. It's 2 AM."

The engineer throws back his head. Shouts at God, "Fuck."

The old man shrugs.

"I jumped ship at Lock Three and cabbed here thinking I'd get an hour on the phone before the ship came, but the fucking cord was cut."

"So you finished her off."

There is no point denying it. The sailor brushes a knife of plastic from his arm with a dramatic gesture, leaving a thin smear of blood on his jacket. "Bell owes me."

"If you say so. What ship you on?"

"The *Douglas Canada*."

"Just one second. Let me check…"

The old man has reached the age when working the lock, pulling cables around and off bollards, is the last appreciable twenty-dollar-an-hour skill he has to offer the world. He is protective of his office. He shuffles into the lock house, a squat, brick building with the architectural refinement of a Hell's Angels clubhouse. Re-emerging a few minutes later, he says, "Yeah." Then: "There's a bank of phones at the bus station, but you'll never make it. You got fifty minutes at most before the *Douglas* gets in. You could get downtown in fifteen…then fifteen back…but you'll need a cab. I don't see one."

The engineer kicks the ground. Attempts the impossible. Tries to forget that whenever one of his phone calls to Halifax finally connects with the woman named Olivia, she might not want him to call.

When he looks up, the line handler still watches, which is awkward. There is nothing more to say, but they are standing too close not to speak. One of them has to talk or one of them has to leave.

The old man speaks first.

"My name's Jerry." The stitching on his pocket confirms it.

"Lucien."

"Don't trust your wife, Lucien?"

"Not married."

Again silence. Jerry pulls a well-used handkerchief from his pocket and indelicately picks his nose. "Bleeding," he observes.

"What?"

"Your hand."

The engineer puts his hand into his pocket.

"Girlfriend?"

The engineer only just catches himself before committing the indignity of confiding a weakness to a stranger, only just stops himself saying, "I was hoping to find out."

A month ago, at Halifax International Airport, a woman the engineer didn't-know-if-he-really-knew made an impossible demand.

"I want you to promise," she said as the last call for his flight was announced, "that for as long as we're doing whatever it is we're doing you won't tell me you love me. Don't write it in a letter."

"No. Let's at least fuck first. When I get back."

"It's not a joke!"

"You're serious?"

"I am serious. I don't like hearing that word. People use it as an expression of disappointment. It ends up trivializing what they feel. I don't want this to be trivial."

"You realize we don't actually know each other."

"Not yet. We don't know where this will go. Maybe we will fall in love. If we do, we won't have to say it. We'll know."

They left it with a kiss so long he had to run to make the flight. Only later, in the coolness of mind that came with his third in-flight rye and ginger—he had a fear of flying—was he struck by the symbolism. In the three weeks since they'd met, love had never come up. Olivia was the first to say the word.

"It's personal," he tells Jerry, although he thinks "preposterous" a better description.

Dismissed, the old man shuffles mechanically to a nearby bollard snow-banked with butts and sits jerkily, like the gears in his knees are missing teeth.

He pulls with yellow fingers an Export A from a green pack with a picture of a beaming girl decked out for sword dancing. Examines his handkerchief closely. Occasionally he coughs for too long.

In the month since Lucien left Olivia at the airport, while the ship steamed mostly between tedious ports in one-bar towns, there were no letters from her, which should have been okay. She wasn't in love; he wasn't in love. Even so, the memory of her kiss was like a life ring in a sea of vacuity. Protection against the numbing rituals of shipboard life. Working twenty feet below the waterline in a steel room. Emerging to the same mess conversations repeated by the same twenty men until they were so slickly polished nothing stuck to them. When the sameness of routines struck him, when he felt utterly alone for being so much the same, he remembered her prohibition. Don't say the word I just said.

Say what then?

He wrote ridiculously long letters addressed to her Tower Street apartment and had the temerity to send them. Every day he worked out new paragraphs, stray sentences, fragments of ideas or events, snippets of conversation. He repeated what he came to realize only after the letters were posted were utterly banal patchworks cut from dull fabric. Things that could mean nothing to a third-year philosophy major at Dalhousie. Like cleaning air intake valves on a compressor and choosing to forgo showering when the ship docked in Sarnia for fear of toxins in the water. His assessment of the new cadet, who'd been put on his watch, who looked like a baby, reeked of high school, and had a ridiculous name.

I told him Harry's a man's name, not a boy's. Was that mean? The sooner he grows up, the safer.

Or the bosun's foray into philosophy:

"All humour is gallows humour because we all know that we're dying"—to which the mate replied, *"What wears a sheet and hides in the sand? The Ku Klux clam. Get it? I made that up when I wasn't thinking about death."*

"It's not funny."

Or the story about the Newfoundland deckhand, Cecil, staring so long at his supper that Bill the cook, also a Newfoundlander, exploded in a fit of indignation.

"Why are you looking at the food that way? You got a problem with it, old cock?"

"Jaysus!—I'm just looking? Can't I look?"

"You weren't just looking. I saw you. You rolled your eyes."

"Roll my—? Now how did I do that?"

"Listen, I saw you. Townie fascist."

"Jaysus!—do you want me to close me eyes from now on? Do you want me to eat with me eyes shut up? If I do, will that shut your trap?"

The pump man said that every meal at home, he had the same conversation with his wife, but in better English.

What could any of that mean to Olivia?

On the *Douglas*, the crew eat meat. If, in the midafternoon, he climbs out of his bunk confused about the calendar, the menu on the galley blackboard is as good as one. Turkey or roast beef means Sunday. Pork chops, Monday. Chicken, Tuesday. Cottage roll, Wednesday. Blood sausages, Thursday (the ship's owner is of Scottish descent, and though he has never set foot on either Scotland or the ship, he insists on adhering to tradition). Fish, Friday. Steak, Saturday.

To prepare him for a three-month stint at sea, Olivia packed a brown paper bag with a peanut butter sandwich and a Tupperware of what looked like seeds. She squinted shyly when handing the lot to him, said, "Oh!" and tossed in an apple.

They are so different. So many things to be said: construction of a life from the blueprint of stories about other people.

No one in the crews' mess, on deck, in the engine room, has noticed him transcribing their lives—scribbling morsels of conversations on napkins and invoices and Bailey charts: anything at hand. On watch, he consults his research. Synthesizes.

Three long, long letters that open him, make his life tangible to her, all signed, *Yours Sincerely, Luci*, have received no reply.

The silence is corrosive.

He's tried phoning. Rehearsed saying things that are exercises in restraint into a finger-thumb receiver. Late one night while the ship crossed the blank face of Lake Ontario under full steam and a quarter moon, Harry caught him practicing, surprised him on watch saying, "We really don't know each other, but I think this is good," to the electrical board.

Lucien quit teasing. A climate of détente prevailed in the engine room.

In Montréal, Port Cartier, and Sarnia, his failed phone calls afflicted him, the silence as thick as a biblical plague. Either she wasn't at home—and she had no answering machine—or she was avoiding him, or was with someone else, someone good-looking she'd met in class, or…the possibilities, whenever he admitted them, were endlessly destructive, which was astonishing considering he wasn't in love and really didn't know her. The courtship had been brief and incomplete.

And so the letters. Written so she would *see* him.

A downbound ship gathers sound in the white. He cranes forward, working out the dimly perceptible pattern of piston strokes.

"You don't hear that anymore," Lucien says.

"I'll find out what it is," says Jerry.

"No need. It's the *Soo River Trader*. That engine runs on steam. There's only one triple expansion left on the lakes."

"It's not loud enough for you to know."

"Triple expansions never get loud: they get vivid."

The old man makes a face into his handkerchief. Blows his nose at the engineer's information. Lucien is reminded of Olivia's initial impression of him.

"You're what I call a machine-brain. People like you don't worry about anyone else's opinion. You have equations."

"Fuck. You."

"Who invited him?"

Sylvia had. Sylvia was a social worker who volunteered answering the suicide hotline in a downtown office. She had been his lover for the better part of five years before they'd given up on romance and moved in together as companionable roommates. She had a breezy, unconnected way with people. Her deepest, dearest friends were all *nice* people. She couldn't come up with any other words for them. That said it all. She'd returned to school after several years wandering professionally in other people's dead ends—pointing the way back—to study philosophy. One day she'd invited him to meet her friends.

"You don't know anyone I know anymore. I've had these friends for two years and you've never met them."

"I'm sure they're nice."

"They are!"

In truth he'd never set foot on the university campus and was fairly certain Dalhousie was a finishing school for effete, middle-class snobs.

He'd sat for lunch with her one day in the undergrad bar. The window where they sat looked out on a patched Pinto, several coats of Bondo giving it the blotchy pattern of a Jersey cow. Three of Sylvia's friends joined their table. In his nervousness, their names evaporated from his consciousness the moment he heard them. He sat mute and stupid, not wishing to reveal his loss. Sylvia introduced Lucien as, "My best friend on rent day, the engineer I didn't marry. I told you all those stories about Luci." Whatever the stories were, no one spoke to him.

Winter had recently given up, the warm weather rubbing out the last lines of ice in public parking lots. The man sitting across the table looked the part of an effete, middle-class snob in his sunbeam-bright yellow scarf, Hawaiian shirt, tartan shorts. He was probably hitting on one of the women; it was hard to tell which. Most likely, the blonde. He spoke his resume, selling himself. No one had heard of his dad who was famous.

The two women were conspicuously different from each other. One was brown, perhaps Indian or Pakistani. She spoke with a Toronto accent, sounded taciturn or bored, or maybe she looked that way. The blonde was effusive, small, garrulous. She spoke at length about her travels in South America, about teaching in Japan. Told a story about being fondled by Japanese grandmothers who wondered at her large tits and perhaps wanted to know how white skin felt. The story, Lucien decided, was "bullshit." He waited for her to say something that would prove it.

"Japan is so strange. You have to go there to get it."

She looked directly at him, and he stirred uncomfortably.

"I'm not into travel."

"Not into travel? You're a sailor."

"They don't build refineries and container docks in the best part of town. The grain elevators are crawling with rats."

"You've heard of taxis."

"Not interested. At least, I don't want to be a tourist. As a kid, I didn't aspire to be one. Maybe you did." That killed her smile. He might have stopped. Instead he said, "People are plastic enough without insisting on them being obsequious for a tip."

"Oh, you know big words."

"I'm not surprised by any of this," said the brown-skinned woman. She dropped a nacho she'd been inspecting for quality back onto the tray. "You're what I call a machine-brain. People like you don't worry about anyone else's opinion. You have equations."

He couldn't stop himself. The Culture Club was playing loudly, his flush of embarrassment soundtracked by Boy George into low comedy. He had to enunciate clearly to be heard exactly properly over the plaintive tones of *Do You Really Want to Hurt Me*.

"Fuck. You."

"Who invited him here?"

The woman who had, Sylvia, watched him stand up and leave. That night she offered an opinion of his behaviour over supper.

"You were an asshole."

He replayed the conversation in his mind. "I'm sorry. I don't like being judged by strangers."

"Who was being judgemental?"

"I was trying to be honest. I don't know how to do that."

"I'll teach you sometime."

But maybe Olivia's right. Listening to the voice of the *Soo River Trader*, he's as good as there. He finds the sounds systematically artful. The remembered smells. Lube oil cooked by steam leaking through packing glands on the main engine and on a multitude of ancillary reciprocating pumps.

A searchlight feels for the concrete wall. Two more line handlers join Jerry, younger men with premature pot bellies, occupational hazard of a job that offers good money for idleness. A black prow knifes through the white. One smooth cut. A voice on deck intones in an Ottawa Valley accent: "*Which hope we have as an anchor of the soul, both sure and steadfast, and which entereth into that within the veil.*"

The three line handlers gaze slack-jawed.

"*Whither the forerunner is for us entered,*" continues the speaker, the Irish or maybe Scottish twang—somewhere in-between, "*even Jesus, made an high priest for ever after the order of Melchisedec.*"

The engineer smiles broadly. "Holy James. Still alive... How did that happen?"

"You know him?" says Jerry.

"I knew him. He won't hurt you. He just wants you to go to heaven."

"Is he crazy?"

"If God's crazy."

"*They that go down to the sea in ships, that do business in great waters; these see the works of the Lord, and His wonders in the deep.*"

The freighter that emerges is 530 feet and encrusted with time, the oldest ship afloat in the Canadian fleet, listing like it has tottered out of Ezekiel's valley of dry bones with a three-day jag on.

"Stop being so loud up there. We're trying to sin."

"Whoa ho!" the voice returns. "Who's that? Luci? Is that you?"

"Hey James."

"It is you, by Gosh! Hey! Hey! How long has it been? You still friends with fornicators?"

"Yeah. You?"

"Don't need 'em. I'm friends with Jesus."

"That's good, James. It's good to have a friend."

"You could have Jesus for a friend, too."

"Maybe I do. Jesus was friends with fornicators."

"Yeah, I guess that's true. But I don't need 'em. Got the love of Jesus."

"What is love?"

"What is what? What kind of halfwit question is that? Love is patient. Love is kind. It does not boast. It is not proud. God is love. Either you know that or you don't, and if you do, you know that love isn't what." He bends over the ship's rail, a rope in his hand. A hooded jogging jacket with white racing stripes covers his coveralls and hardhat like a Kmart cowl. He gestures about. "It's how much."

The telegraph sounds from the engine room gangway door. The pistons change speed, the prop frothing the water as the ship slows. James tosses the rope attached to a cable to Jerry. Then, tethered like a giant Gulliver in a pint-sized world, the ship waits in the lock, vibrating deeply. The ship descends, disappears. The doors open on the bow-end of the lock. The ship's horn blasts and the line handlers let loose the cables from the bollards. The *Soo River Trader* disappears downbound into the fog.

"*Then they cry unto the Lord in their trouble, and he bringeth them out of their distresses. He maketh the storm a calm, so that the waves thereof are still. Then are they glad because they be quiet; so he bringeth them unto their desired haven.* That there, that's love, Luci. *When the trumpet of the Lord shall sound, and time shall be no more. Safe and secure from all alarms.*"

By three Lucien and Jerry have sat through the comings and goings of two ships, lakers heading for ports on Huron or Superior, Michigan, Erie. Lucien has been writing a thought letter.

> *Dear Olivia,*
>
> *I ran into my first love today—the ship I sailed on when I was eighteen. My leaving-home boat—the* Soo River Trader. *I lost my virginity on the* Trader. *I was in a bar in Duluth and I met this married woman who was familiar with the alleys. After that, my best friend in the crew called me "the fornicator." He was religious. Everyone else was congratulatory. I must have boasted.*

It's as impossible as the real letters. He is struck by the inability to even imagine writing to a woman who does not reply. The more she disappears into a haze of supposition, the greater his captivity.

The fog thinning, through a gap along the upbound shore, a ship emerges dragging smoke.

"That's her," says Lucien.

He has to admit that for all the labour, isolation, disappointment, anxiety, and depression it demands and causes, the approaching ship is handsome by any sailor's standards. Constructed of sharp angles to cut the sea and painted red to cut the sky, the bow is pointed, not bulbous—the current style. It looks more than seaworthy, looks Jack London-worthy.

A voice calls out from the deck, "That you Luci?"

"Yeah."

"I'll get the gangway."

The passage from shore to ship is quick. In the time it takes the *Douglas* to settle, two deckhands slide a gangway that angles steeply from the ship to shore, the angle lessening fast as the water runs through the lower lock door and the ship descends. When the deck is nearly parallel to the lip of the lock, Lucien boards.

Wandering into the after house, he is met by the Lurker, a forty year-old chain smoker, whose talent is for blowing smoke rings without having a cigarette in his hand. No one is ever impressed.

"Did you get your mail?" says the Lurker.

"What mail?"

"From the post office at Lock Three."

"Missed it. Went ashore at Lock Three to use the phone. Where is it?"

"The cook said you were waiting for something and he'd put it in your cabin."

"That's considerate."

The Lurker makes a face. Whatever his real name is, no one on the ship uses it. "He knew you'd wake him up if he didn't. Your hand bleeding?"

He checks. "No, it stopped."

In his cabin, Lucien finds the letter on his bed, an odd shaped affair with Olivia's return address. He rips into it to find a Hi Fi chromium dioxide cassette labeled "Lucien: attempt #3." He shifts the mess on his dresser and retrieves a Walkman, flips out a copy of *Remain in Light*, replacing it with Olivia's cassette. The batteries are dead.

No one in the passageway. The galley closed. The Lurker gone. Lucien, roams the deck fore and aft, hunting for anyone who can help, hears a whistled song from the amidships pipe shop. Jack, the 12-4 watchman, has *Heartbreak Hotel* stuck in his head again.

"I need double-A batteries."

"Yeah, I've got some, but I want them replaced. Money's no good. It doesn't pay for the time it takes to go ashore and find an open store. I want batteries for batteries."

"Anything. Where are they?"

"Top dresser drawer. Don't disturb anything."

Lucien ducks back into the after house. Jack's cabin is on the lower level starboard side. It is the first time Lucien has been in it, and when he enters he is surprised by a facet of the watchman he'd been unaware of. Jack isn't just bivouacked in his cabin, as Lucien is in his; he is nesting, the bulkheads decorated to suit his tastes.

On the bum boats in his travels and in shit-ports, Jack has managed to lay hands on an impressive library of pornographic images. They are cut into shape and taped to the cabin's four bulkheads. None of the women is identifiable, not a single pair of eyes peers back from the cold, green steel. Jack's fetishism has edited their bodies to a series of parts: vulvas, asses. They are unrecognizable as anything but objects to be penetrated. Indeed, some of the body parts are pictured in the act of being penetrated; there are close-ups of penises entering women's mouths (the photographs edited decisively at the base of the nose by Jack's scissors), women's vaginas and elsewhere. All the faceless lips seem to whisper Jack's name.

He feels into the top dresser drawer, finds the batteries. Then he is back in his cabin, with its yellow-stained walls from the countless smokers who've held his rank and slept and awoken in his cot. He drops onto the lizard-green settee bolted to the deck beneath the cabin's only porthole. Pulls up his legs, crossing them under his body, the way schoolchildren sometimes sit at their desks when they've overcome their fear of the teacher.

Eyes closed, he listens to Olivia's voice. On a 90-minute cassette she has spoken three words.

"I love you."

2. April–June

"Halifax was once a sailors' city. Now it's a city of passengers. In the future, the restaurants will be more important than the people. Five years from now, you won't be able to buy a loaf of bread on Spring Garden Road."
—Said on Hollis Street by a prostitute to a regular.

SIX DAYS AFTER the Welland Canal, the ship against a wall in Sorel.

In instructor mode, Lucien daytrips into town with Harry, buys two Laurentides at a dépanneur and demonstrates how to use the curb to pry the caps off.

"All the world is a bottle opener," he lectures.

Harry has been given to Lucien as an engine room cadet after proving unteachable on every other watch. He is a short, boyish man with thick, black hair and dramatic eyes. His resting expression is a look of bewildered credulity, like he's besieged by an inchoate worldliness. It puzzles Lucien why anyone so deficient of mechanical inclination would want to be an engineer. Mostly having given up on the mentorship assignment, he is teaching Harry how to drink.

Gilles Villeneuve is dead, as a black and white photograph of him in his coffin taped to a drugstore window attests. He's been dead since May, killed in a crash in Belgium. Lucien wonders at the Elvis-level of reverence. In the picture, Villeneuve is dressed in his Formula 1 outfit, his helmet and driving gloves on his knees, like a Viking chief, bearing needed things to the afterlife.

At a bar called La Terrasse Picardie they order drinks and watch women stroll the sidewalk.

"That girl," says Harry, "I've seen her before somewhere."

"Don't kid yourself that you know anyone here. If you're going to be a sailor you'll have to get used to being anonymous."

Harry sees her twice more before his beer is half finished. "She's doing the block over and over."

"Walking a dog."

"An invisible dog." It's not just her. "Tight, black pants, white shirt, jean jacket. See her? The one with the big bag."

Lucien is convinced he's seen someone in that outfit before. Thin and blonde. Somewhere.

"The two behind. They're doing laps."

Lucien shrugs. "Every town has its customs. Try not to be a tourist." He holds up his glass. "Be a drinker."

While they finish their beers they count the coming-and-goings of a dozen women, all in their late teens or early twenties. The women don't speak. Don't look up. The day is warm and bright and they're walking.

"We're in Stepford," says Harry.

"It's just people walking. It doesn't mean anything."

"Everything means something."

"No. Some things just happen."

In the park across the street a fair is setting up. They wander over and stop at a yellow VW Van converted into a gypsy caravan with blue blankets and tinfoil moons and stars. A man reads tarot for ten bucks. He is emaciated and bent and has a hooked nose that looks prosthetic. He wears a Satan's Choice jacket sporting a decal of a toothy, grinning red devil with flames for hands.

Lucien is disappointed with his reading.

"Stay away from waters," the man says. "Waters will kill you."

They walk back to the ship. Buy another round of Laurentides and open them on a mailbox and a fencepost.

"He knew I was a sailor the minute he looked at my hands," Lucien tells Harry.

He holds them up. His nails, the pores of his fingers, perma-stained black with Bunker C.

"All the world's a bottle opener," Harry replies and they toast.

Seven weeks earlier, his face pressed in a novel in a bar in Scotia Square, Lucien was surprised by someone tapping his book with a dayglo fingernail. Interrupting his reading of an engrossing passage about an English ambassador in Quauhnahuac, Mexico pissing on his neighbour's lawn.

"You're really into that. We've been at the next table for two drinks trying to decide if that was your forehead."

The fingernail belonged to Sylvia's blonde friend, as did Princess Di bangs, Celtic cross earrings, and an expression that could have come from a Maybelline ad, her smile that stoned. She was dressed in tight pastels: pink pants, periwinkle shirt. Behind her the testy woman tipped her beer in a mock toast and nodded pleasantly-enough as though his attitude at their first meeting was forgotten.

"We couldn't see your face."

"I'm sorry. I don't remember…"

"My name? Cathy. Olivia's the one you told to fuck off. How did you say it? Like two sentences? Fuck. Off. Is that how sailors swear? I've heard they're experts. Tell me to shove it up my ass."

Someone else might have appeared a smudge in her outfit. Cathy looked fit, looked like she had completed a degree in *Jane Fonda's Advanced Workout*. The tightness of her shirt proved yesterday's admission about the size of her tits.

A waiter with a loaded tray stopped. "We don't swear in this restaurant."

Cathy shrugged and said, "Oops." Then: "Is this how you spend your time? Reading in dark bars?"

It was.

"Don't you have better things to do with your time and money? I know sailors make money hand over fist. My cousin deckhands—is that a word?—on a harbour tug. He's never out of port for more than half a day and he owns two canoes and a Harley. Why aren't you out somewhere buying something?"

"I suck at being middle class."

He'd been trying for the better part of ten years to figure out how it worked, but the math was impressionistic. Being a sailor meant leading a double life and living half of one. His shore friends lived with the continuity of a movie. His life was a slide show. He was here. He was there. His rent cheque, not any sense of inclusion, made him a Haligonian. As an afternoon ritual, he'd settled on a number of bars in which to read. Dick Turpin's Pub was an upstairs bar at the base of the Chateau Halifax decorated and darkened to look like a basement, and frequented by wags who called it Dic Purpin's Tub. The carpet smelled faintly of mold. His walk home after a one-beer read often randomly guided by whatever lights were green, might take twenty minutes or an hour, but the end was always the same: wiping his shoes on the mat before standing aimlessly in front of an open fridge, his mind stupefied with depression.

"Will you join us?"

He stuffed a coaster into his novel to hold the page, sat beside her, across from the short-tempered woman.

"You sure know how to focus. Two good looking girls sit down next to you and you don't look up." Cathy took his book. "Malcom Lowry? Don't know him. I'm into Anne Rice. Have you read her?"

"Is she good?"

"Good? First book I ever read that made me want to fuck a vampire." She touched his hand.

A man with a guitar entered from the mall and approached the stage—a parquetted four by four square that in any bar in the Lower Townships would have been reserved for strippers.

"Crap," said Lucien.

"What?" Olivia stirred.

"He's going to play *Jimmy's Dream*."

"How do you know?"

"Anyone who sings off-key plays *Jimmy's Dream*."

"I'll bet he doesn't," said Olivia.

"He will because everyone wants him to. It appeals to people who associate sophistication with Toronto. The worse it's played, the louder they applaud."

"I'm from Toronto."

"I'll keep your secret."

She crossed her arms. "I'll bet he doesn't."

The waiter stopped—he'd been stopping a lot at their table, never at Lucien's—and Olivia ordered a stout.

The man with the guitar adjusted the microphone and coughed. He looked fifty or an unhealthy forty, wore faded jeans and a checked shirt. He scanned the room like a curmudgeon looking for something to improve. "Forgive my nerves," he said, "I've never played in public." His guitar had the rub of an instrument either beloved or second-hand. "This is a song I learned how to play in the kitchen." He smiled broadly, cuing the audience to smile back. He sang,

Jimmy, I need you at home
Don't go fishin' on that boat
while the capelin's a runnin'
and the trawlers' a comin'
from Spain...

"Crap is right," said Olivia. "Learned how to play in the john not the kitchen."

By the time the set ended with a smattering of polite, embarrassed applause at the end of an indifferent rendition of *Barrett's Privateers*, Lucien was on his third beer.

"You should have taken my bet," Olivia said.

She wasn't flashy. Unlike Cathy, Olivia dressed for playing bingo. The other Sylvia-friends he'd met were openly formulaic, leading lives imitative of the conventions of romantic comedy. The ring finger of Olivia's right hand looked like it had been snapped and set improperly. She followed his eyes and put her hand into her pocket.

"What do you have that I'd want?" he asked. "Sorry. Is that rude?"

"Yes," they both said.

"I'm sorry. I don't know about people. That's one of the reasons I sail. Most of the time, I'm talking to one person, my oiler, who works with me. I like that. I don't want to offend anyone. I find talking to strangers, especially strangers who are friends, like playing a game I can't understand because the rules are in Latin. I can't explain. You'll have to forgive me for being stupid. But I'm not a conversationalist."

"But you're *not* stupid," said Olivia. "Are you? You just don't know when to stop talking."

"I think it's best for everyone if I stop now."

Twenty minutes later and Cathy was beginning to sound mildly shitfaced.

"Dave's nowhere near as provocative as he pretends," she said. "His political convictions are consistent with someone who uses whoopee as a noun." How long had she been talking and who was Dave? He noticed that even when Cathy wasn't talking about sex she was talking about sex.

"I go pee now." She stood up unsteadily. He silently tick-tocked the metre of her walk, tried to decide if the generous way she swung her hips was in any sense a character trait and, if it was, what it said about her. He wondered how to find out. He'd been at sea for a long time. And he felt a dull anger at himself for being irresolute, saw that Cathy returned from the bathroom wearing fresh lipstick. Olivia excused herself. He had time now for a pitch, any pitch. She smiled a say-anything smile that silenced him.

She said, "Do you know how to flirt? If you want a woman to think you're flirting put a soupçon of interest and energy into your conversation. It actually doesn't take very much these days, everyone is so dedicatedly bored."

The directness deepened his freeze. He thought about how best to breathe. When, after a half minute, he hadn't spoken, she offered, "You can call me Cath."

"That's good." He stroked his beer, caught himself at it, and stopped.

"Not much of a short form, I know. Do you wish my parents had called me Cynthia?"

Olivia returned to the table wearing fresh lipstick.

The next afternoon while Sylvia social-worked they fucked. He marveled at the smell of her skin, the touch of her naked chest, the sound of her breath. He was okay with her biting his shoulder. Afterwards they lay together, their clothes in two heaps beside the bed, one blue and black, the other mauve.

It was Cathy's plan. While Olivia was settling the tab, she pulled a pen from her purse. Looked around for the first paper product she could find, tugged the coaster out of his book, and wrote her number on it. Then she slipped it back at random and looked round to see if Olivia had noticed. She put a dayglo finger to her lips but she didn't need to.

That night, Sylvia made supper as a trade for him listening to her story about a phone call at work from the sort of man she would never allow into her house but who she was helping to get into counselling. He half-listened, his mind feverish with the details of an encounter yet to happen.

"The issue," Sylvia had told him, "is always the same. I'm helping people whose depression has landed them smack in the centre of the universe. Everything is happening to them. The issue is cosmological. There is no such thing as coincidence. Their depression has rendered them utterly arrogant. That's what depression does when it reaches a certain pitch."

"Or," he said, "it does the opposite. Some people are hollowed out. They want to do service. They want to give themselves up to helping people."

"Example?"

"You. When you're depressed you're a saint without a religion. All sacrifice and no reward."

He didn't catch the effect of this on Sylvia, who rubbed her ear with an expression of befuddlement. She picked up her fork, pressed patterns in her mashed potatoes. She flipped her hair to demonstrate her interest in continuing the conversation but he was elsewhere. He was imagining Cathy naked.

Maybe she just wanted to be friends, or maybe she was mocking him, paying him back for his tourist remark. Maybe if he invited her over she wouldn't show up.

His maybes were unconvincing.

When Sylvia left home in the morning, he retrieved the coaster, took a deep breath, and dialed.

"I'm home today, if you want to come over and...um...talk."

"Where's Sylvia? Not in class."

"Working till five."

"Okay. I'm coming over now, but let's not talk. You have a bad habit of telling women to fuck off. Let's just do it."

Afterwards she said, "I don't know anything about you except Sylvia's stories from which I presume you're Doctor Livingstone."

"Sylvia! What would she think of all this?"

"She'd hate me. Try not to tell her. She wants you back."

"Does not."

"I am baffled by your blindness. I find it sweet. Never mind. Don't complicate this. So, tell me something else about your life and interests. You're a sailor who spends his free time reading in bars. Do you have a pet fish?"

"Not even a plant. Nothing that needs regular care. I'm only home four months a year."

"Is there anything else you do with those months besides read in bars?"

What did he do?

"I go to art galleries."

"You are sooo interesting. A machine-brain—is that what Olivia calls you?—at the art gallery. Explain. Are you one of those guys who reads the plate on the bottom of the picture to figure out how old the artist lived before committing suicide by alcohol and never looks at the paintings?"

"I'm the other kind. I go to see one piece of art. Then I leave."

"Fabulous! How long do you spend on your one piece of art?"

"Maybe twenty minutes. It depends. I always see a different work."

"Perfect. Now tell me why."

"Because I don't get it."

"Don't get what?"

"Art. Stop laughing at me. You asked so I'm telling. I know when I'm looking at art, like when I'm sailing by Quebec City at twilight. The view's impressive from the river, but I can't put it together as anything else. It just doesn't happen for me."

"Ha! I love it. Tell me, what's your favourite colour?"

He might have stopped, but she was too good looking, especially naked with her chin propped on an arm propped on his chest.

"When I sail past the Chateau Frontenac I see geometry. Buildings here. Cliffs here. Sunset. Water. I can memorize it like I'm studying for a history test but I can't feel it."

"You're aware that you don't have an empathetic response to art? Just knowing that about yourself makes you refreshingly strange. By the way, the first rule of art appreciation is to blame the artist for anything you don't get. The second is until you've toured the Sistine Chapel don't say you go to art galleries. Not until you've embraced the doctrines of tourism. Anyway, have you considered that the problem might be that you *are* an artist? Artists are forever asking themselves why they did it."

"I don't want to ask that question. I want to be the answer to it. I want to say to the artist, say to God if there is one, I'm the reason you did it. *I* get it. But I don't. I don't get any of it. I think it might be okay if someone were with me, someone else witnessing and taking pleasure from it. I could feel that—someone else's…feeling. I think that's the worst thing about my job. I'm like a deaf patron at the symphony. I wouldn't know when to applaud. Hey, do you want to see something with me sometime?"

Cathy said, "You are so accident prone."

"What did I do?"

"You didn't have to do anything. I just listen to you and I hear accidents. You exude them like I exude sex. That's not vanity. It's measurable. I see men staring. No, we're definitely not meant to be together."

"Did I offend you?"

"No."

"But you don't like me."

"I like you but it won't work."

"You think I'm shallow?"

"I don't care about that. Think of me as an action girl," she wiggled her ass, "a cunt who knows her Kant. What Kant tells me is you need someone else. Actually, that's coming from Sartre. Even Olivia would be better than me."

She reached between his legs and tickled him hard. He wouldn't have guessed that was possible. He said, "Wait? You want to do me again after saying we're not suited?"

She shrugged, wriggled down his body, arched her back, licked his belly button. "You can stop me."

"I refuse."

"Then I will."

Cathy positioned her hips over his and whispered conspiratorially, "Let's not say anything about this to anyone. We can give each other shameful looks across the bar from time to time when Sylvia's not looking. She'd be devastated if she found out." She winked, pulled him just into her, thrust her body down hard, and gasped.

After she left, he walked to the harbour and tracked the waves, watched them bend into the shore with liquid roar and disappear. He tried to get a bead on where they began. He shuddered at the memory of telling Cathy about art galleries and Quebec. He felt ashamed, not angry. How many times had Sylvia told him he was weird? He knew he was off every time he signed ships articles, every time he stood at a captain's desk, pen in hand and a foot in the 19th Century.

He tossed a stone at a breaker and thought about Cathy. There was something palpably fragile about her will to transgression. He thought she was right. Their sex was everything it could be. It wasn't enough. He would never love her and he wanted to be in love. Not in the protective way he loved Sylvia, but in the way of something inevitable and overwhelming.

He arrived the next night to a Prince Street bar decorated to look like a bar: faux license plates, movie posters, lobster traps, a life preserver from the *S.S. Minnow*. Cathy, Olivia, Sylvia, and the man who he assumed was Dave half-held a table that was also half-held by four barely-legal-looking possibly-first-years, who appeared in their natural element with the dim lights and throbbing bassline.

"Hey, it's the machine-man," said maybe Dave.

Sylvia looked perplexed.

"Who invited you?"

"We did," said Cathy and Olivia.

She looked more perplexed.

"We ran into him a couple days ago at Dick Turpin's. Didn't we tell you?" said Olivia.

She shook her head. "I'm glad you're pals. I feel responsible for Lucien. To the best of my knowledge, he has no friends." She patted his back.

"What's not to like?" said Cathy. She wore tight, black pants and a white shirt, accessorizing with a jean jacket draped casually over a Birkinesque bag. "He's so afraid of the sound of his own voice he makes an excellent conversationalist."

Sylvia eyed her closely. "Okay."

The bar was loaded like a cannon. Dancers rubbed against each other on a raised platform fenced with a rail. Others looking depressed roamed the room, competing streams pushing against each other to no discernible purpose, exchanging *sorry*s. Lucien observed the way Sylvia spoke, her possessive mannerism of turning to him for confirmation—not of her statements, but their import—as couples did when their ability to hold conversations was defeated by the quiet suppression of safe, unimportant stories. After a couple beers, he excused himself and wedged to the bathroom. Standing in line, he was surrounded by preppy men in orange and yellow. The bathroom stank of body odour and Brut.

On his way back to the table he observed Cathy's arched posture as she leaned across their table. The four possibly-first-years shook with laughter, their eyes freely roaming Cathy's ass. He felt vaguely stupid watching her pose for them.

Sylvia and maybe Dave were arguing Free Trade. Olivia smiled nervously. She'd dressed for clubbing in a way that suggested she didn't do much of it: flower print sundress, black mules. She was cautiously made up, competently mascaraed.

He smiled nervously back, decided it would be best not to speak. No point getting into trouble. They sat looking away from each other for an interminable minute.

Olivia broke first. "I bought your book."

"My book?"

"The one you were reading. *Under the Volcano*. I've just started."

"Don't blame me if you don't like it."

"I like it."

He said, "Good. You could swim in its mood."

"What?"

The possibly-first-years had ratcheted up the volume. Maybe Dave was pounding the table and digging up Trudeau: "I, for one, don't want an elephant rolling over me."

"I said, oh, never mind." Lowering his voice he added, "I'm scared of you, too."

She shrugged and pointed to her ears. He nodded. They politely looked away, but he found himself returning to look at her. Her resting expression was a pout. She had full lips that lent theatricality to her evident disdain. She might have been sucking on an olive. Behind her, Cathy was chugging. A line of beer ran down her neck.

"I suspect you are the most interesting person in this bar," he said and he meant it although the information surprised him. He added, "For all I know, you may even be beautiful."

The possibly-first-years stopped laughing and the onslaught of sound abated.

Olivia turned sharply, smiled, and shrugged. People jostled past. He bent to accommodate them.

"Wait," she shouted. "Who's beautiful?"

"I said..."

The possibly-first-years opened up with another salvo of laughter, forcing Lucien to retreat into pantomime. He pointed to his mouth. Even still, he could feel what she could see: the barometer of his embarrassment. Reddening.

Later, he discovered Olivia staring at him intently with an alarmed expression of interest.

At closing, the bar spilled onto Prince Street. A mumbling man courted the crowd for change. "For coffee," he explained. Olivia pulled a one dollar bill from her purse, thought better of it, and put a two into the man's hand. They continued down the street. Still in earshot of the man, maybe Dave said, "He's going to spend it on alcohol."

"That's what I'd do if I were him."

They walked down Prince towards the water, trying to keep a straight sidewalk. At the corner of Barrington, Cathy said, "Bon voyage *bon vivants*," and fell into the street.

Maybe Dave helped her up. "I'll get her home." He read Sylvia and Olivia's expressions and said, "Just that. I promise. I'll get her to bed and leave. What? Okay. Okay. I'll get her to the door of her apartment and leave."

"We'll all go," said Sylvia.

"Not me," said Lucien.

"Turning in?"

"Walking."

"Looking for art or just the meaning of life?"

"I don't want to waste all the money I've spent on booze going to sleep."

"Feeling frugal?"

"I'll come," said Olivia. "I drank twenty bucks."

Sylvia was stuck. The corners of her mouth showed she knew it.

The streets were emptying out except Hollis where the prostitutes were holding court, waiting for their peak business hour after the cabarets closed. Olivia said, "Hi," to a brown-skinned woman across from the post office, who was more spandexed than Pat Benatar and, for want of a sweatband, less dressed. She returned the "Hi" and winked.

They continued to the waterfront. The night was overcast and a shore bound breeze touched gently, coolly. They sat on the edge of a wharf listening to waves plashing the posts below their feet. The sea smell soothed. They smiled at each other anxiously. Olivia looked like someone trying to suppress a shiver.

"Is this what it's like to be a sailor?" She took off her shoes and gestured with a foot to the water just below the reach of her toes.

He remembered the lesson of Cathy: don't say anything that could be construed as poetic.

"I don't usually get that close to the water. It's more like that." He pointed to the refinery across the water at Eastern Passage, a blaze of light spotlighting cranes and tanks.

"Not very romantic."

"In movies. Being a sailor puts one in mind of time. It's like living with a calendar with missing months." He cursed himself for breaking his rule.

"Listen. I was wrong about you and I'm sorry. When we met, you acted like a prick. I imagined you must be self-absorbed like the rest of Sylvia's friends."

"I worried you were nice."

She rubbed her arms.

"I didn't dress for this. I expected to be ignored by drunk strangers for an hour and go home. If I'd known this would be an option, I'd have brought my parka."

He ran through a quick inventory of things not to say, like, "You'd probably look hot in a parka."

"Okay," she said to his silence. She looked at him closely. Rubbed her crooked finger. "Should we exchange numbers? No, forget it. Let's agree that if we want to talk, we'll look for each other here."

They didn't touch, didn't kiss.

The next night at the same time he sat in the same place looking into the same patterns. The darkness of near-dark—clouds reflecting city lights. Points of white across the bay stifled on the right edge of vision by McNabs Island, a blackening like a blind spot on the periphery. Voices ashore and at sea: bar sounds; the muffled conviviality of a schooner running on engine power. The green starboard light of a tug returning alone to port.

When she arrived, she took off her shoes again, but this time she was wearing socks. She'd brought a sweater.

She talked about her classes. She talked about being a shitty soccer player when she was five. She talked about being afraid of birds flying overhead but being unafraid of spiders and mice and skunks. About being enamoured of blue glass, about a family trip to India. He could feel her self-doubt. Her words accumulated around him. Squinting shyly, she told him about three high school friends who'd gotten into a car with a drunk driver, talked about their funerals. She talked about her family.

"My parents immigrated just before I was born. They hate everything Canadian. I was raised on disapproval. Even today when I'm stuck in traffic I can hear my dad, the philosopher king of the road, shouting at the windshield: *Out of the way boondi brain*, or, *Have another ladoo, road pig*. Sheesh, the drivers aren't better in India. It's like having to remember to breathe—I have to remind myself not to dislike people. What's bred in the bone...I'm sorry. This isn't interesting."

"Sounds like Protestant guilt. Everyone else is a sinner. Only you and your best friends from high school are saved. That's the stuff I was raised on. Except I've never known my parents to be angry."

"I suppose you'll say that's just as bad."

He reminded himself not to talk. "I won't. It isn't."

"You grew up not wanting to be a tourist. What else? Did you live by the water?" He hadn't. "Did you dream of being a sailor and going to refineries, container docks, and grain elevators?"

26

"I grew up on a farm. And I didn't want anything to do with water." He could feel his resolve to be normal slipping. "I used to have a recurring dream that I drowned. I could taste the water."

"You're not supposed to die in dreams."

"Well I didn't know that when I was three. I'm here for the mechanics, not the romance. It was the first thing I picked up on. The sound, smell, power of machines. Even the danger. A few good horsepower can kill you or be part of a beautiful system and I like systems. So when I was eighteen I signed into a college program in marine engineering, not to go to sea—that was incidental— but because I wanted to work on big engines. Anything bigger than me. 10,000 horse power, four cylinder Sulzers. Steam ships. Turbines."

He was staring at her socks. Watching her feet work slow circles above the water.

He said, "I think something has changed. Weird that it could happen so fast."

She followed his gaze and stopped her feet.

"Yes," she said. "Jane Austen could learn a thing or two from us. Not that we're a couple. We don't know each other."

What did he know? He knew she was twenty-one. He knew she was brown and he was white. He'd given it enough thought the previous night to know he could make nothing of it. No one he knew was in a mixed-race relationship, and the examples on TV were few and risqué. He still didn't know what he wanted.

On their first official date they sat across from each other at a bar on Granville, both reading *Under the Volcano*. He was within a half-inch of the ending. On his page, the English ambassador in Mexico was in trouble, acting on his feelings. He didn't know what page she was on, just that she was two thirds in and that every time he looked up she was watching, calculating, he supposed. At least, he wanted her to do that.

Years earlier, mid-way through Lucien's long relationship with Sylvia he'd been awoken one night by voices outside, anger in the street, bar-closing taunts. He felt an unconstrained dread. The window was moonlit, nothing in view on the sidewalk below. He returned to bed, into the half-light, and scanned Sylvia's half-shadowed profile. What he didn't see of her features, he remembered.

It came on him suddenly, surprising him, fear that his pseudo-marriage to Sylvia had committed him to a permanent state of absence. He couldn't say who she really was.

He began the slow process of letting her break up with him. In the two years that followed, he wouldn't do anything specific to bring about the end. He caused their breakup by willing it, the way the aged will death when they feel they're used up, when they become invisible to other people.

A week after their first official date, as they sat at the harbour, Olivia said, "Whatever it is we're starting, and I do want to start something, I want it to start honest. So…that's what I'm doing. I'm going to tell you something that's not very good. And I'm not going to apologize for it. I'm just going to tell it."

"What's it about?"

For the first time since they'd started their quiet dates he worried about his tryst with Cathy. Maybe not important. Definitely difficult to broach.

Olivia fussed with her finger. Bent it straight. Was defeated by its crookedness.

"No. I can't tell it. We have to know each other first." She shook her head, preoccupied herself again with her finger. "I'll talk to Maud. She'll know. I'm sure she's told people worse things."

"Who's Maud?"

"My cousin. You saw her. When we left the bar last week."

"Don't remember."

"She's the brains of the family."

"What's she do?"

"Prostitutes." She glanced towards the necklace of lights across the water. "I don't know why she does that."

"I assume it's not charity. She gets paid."

"She could do other things. She's a genius. Don't worry, prostitution is not hereditary."

It struck Lucien as a categorical oddity. He'd never known anyone with a prostitute for a cousin. "A hooker named Maud? How Victorian."

Everyone in his family farmed.

"She's not just that. No one is. When I first moved into town she came to see me and she's tried to be a confidante ever since. I don't know how she knew I was here; I'd forgotten about her."

"But she wants to be chums?"

"She calls sometimes. She's persistent. She told me a story the first time we had tea. She said that on the day I came home from the hospital my mother put me in her lap and said I was her present. Maud would have been nine. There I was, her living doll. Imagine. My first memory of Maud is her putting a dress on me. I couldn't get my arms in the right holes. That's why she wants to be chums. She won't break faith with the girl she was before she got into trouble.

"She's here recovering or hiding. Bad Toronto influences. Maud says when I have problems I'm to come to her. I do think she'd be protective as a bear if I let her be, but I don't know. Something about her isn't right... Sorry. Sorry. This is not what we're talking about. We're talking about openness. When I can, I'll tell you a story. Whatever we're doing, we have to know each other, and as much as I don't want it to be, the story is about me."

"Okay," he said. "Why don't you ask something about me? Ask anything you think is important. You decide what matters."

"Why aren't you married to Sylvia? What didn't you like?"

"I didn't like feeling dead."

"That's it exactly. Yeah. Being with Maud is like being with someone who feels dead. That's what scares me. Don't ever allow yourself to feel dead."

The first time they kissed was at the Halifax International Airport. He'd woken up that morning in his new apartment in the North End to a voice on the phone that was one week early.

"What do you mean you've booked my flight? My time's not up."

"It is if you want your job."

"What happened to my relief?"

"Well, he quit. Turns out, he thought the work would be supervisory like on his last ship. Apparently he worked for Fischer Price Marine on the *Good Ship Lollipop*."

"That wasn't a ship."

"He didn't want to do repairs and the chief insisted. We can't hire someone else for just one week."

"Fuck."

"So, for the record, are you coming or are you unemployed?"

"When's the flight?"

"2:20."

His apartment wasn't put together: his bedroom a Tetris of still-packed liquor store boxes that he had to negotiate to find a coffee maker. Even with the clutter, the just-rented cleanliness of the apartment made him long for a cat.

Finding a new apartment had been a cinch. Explaining his reasons to Sylvia hadn't been as hard as he'd imagined when he came home twice from talk-dates with Olivia to discover subtle alterations in his room. What had convinced him to leave was the evidence that Sylvia had been inspecting his bed, searching for clues on the sheets.

"I'm thirty next week," he said to her, "and thirty-year-olds don't have roommates."

By the time he'd found the coffee pot and hunted down a bag of grounds packed in a Captain Morgan's box with a tennis racket and shoes, it was 10 AM. He'd been stupid with time or he'd been allowing the news to sink in before telephoning Olivia.

"I don't think you're going to like what I have to tell you," he said on the phone. "Personally, I hate it."

"Okay. Tell me." She sounded sleepy.

"I have to go. I've been called back to the ship. I'm flying to Quebec this afternoon."

"What?"

"I'm sorry. I know it's quick. I don't get to decide."

There was a long silence during which he thought the background sounds seem to change as though she were walking towards and away from a buzzing refrigerator or air conditioner.

Again she said, "What?"

"It's time. I have to go."

More silence.

"Olivia?"

"Come over. Tower Street Apartments." She gave him the address.

"I still have to pack."

"Do that. But bring your luggage and leave from here."

They had maybe half an hour in her apartment, a bachelor done up in plants. He grasped her life in it from absences. No kitchen table meant she probably ate on the bed. No TV, radio, or record player meant she didn't need a constant drone of sound around her. No clocks meant he worried about missing his plane.

"I knew you would have to go, but I didn't know how it would feel. I thought I had another week to prepare myself." She wandered back and forth past a fridge that periodically chattered and hummed, huffed and fell silent.

"I have to make you lunch."

"There's no need."

"Don't argue." She turned to him with an expression that begged sympathy. "I have to give you something to take."

From a breadbox on the counter she removed and half-unpacked a loaf of bread, purposefully taking two slices from the middle. The butter she spread precisely, ensuring she left no uncovered borders. She had a curious way with the knife, like it wasn't a utensil but a paint brush. When the butter was exactly even, she paused to consider her work. She carried out the same exact process with the peanut butter. The procedure took time, during which Olivia did not speak. She was drawn into herself, breathing.

When she finished she wrapped the sandwich in Saran Wrap, fetched a Tupperware from the drawer beside the sink and filled it from a bag on the counter. She packed a brown paper bag and sized it up as though it were a business letter that needed to faithfully fit its envelope. She closed it with a straight fold.

"No. I want to see you off. I just think there's something that has to be said and I can't think. It's too quick. You haven't given me enough time." Her eyes were edged with tears of frustration.

"Oh!"

"What is it? What's wrong?"

She went to the fridge, took an apple from the crisper, and dropped it into the bag.

In the airport she told him another story.

"Airports scare me. Not because of the planes, but because of what they might be carrying. Grief. I was in Pearson a couple years ago waiting for my mother's plane. I was sitting at a bank of chairs and the whole row but my seat was filled with a single, silent family. They were behaving so strangely but I didn't know what it was that made them strange until I realized they never looked at each other. They were consciously avoiding each other's expressions. Grief has a posture. It doesn't sit well or still. It bobs. The plane landed. The passengers deplaned, a line of mud faces preoccupied with making connections or retrieving luggage or finding a payphone, a taxi. The usual crush. There's no face like the face of someone deplaning. Most of the crowd had passed when a half dozen sombre-dressed passengers, the youngest in her teens and the oldest a grandfather, came through the gate and locked eyes on the group sitting beside me. The moment they did, it was as though a starter's pistol had fired. Everyone burst in tears. The combined wail... I could feel it inside me like I was a consort to their grief. I think about it now every time I'm in an airport. I look at people's faces and wonder when it will start, that cry, carried like luggage from somewhere unexpected."

Why was her expression so fierce?

"I want you to promise that for as long as we're doing whatever it is we're doing you won't tell me you love me. Don't write it in a letter."

A pinched voice announced his flight.

When they kissed, the fear surrounding him was of tomorrow and the next day and a week or month later. All fear was of later. The calm cool immediacy of his feelings, the open honesty of her kiss: that was now.

She held him tight, whispered in his ear, "I don't know you."

Harry says, "Aren't you old not to be married?"

They're in view of home, dimly. Across a brown street on a side where no one has bothered to build a house, barely visible above a weed-tangled hill is a geometric arrangement of wires and poles that belongs to the tanker beneath.

"You're never too old not to be married."

"I'm going to get married before I turn thirty."

"What's the rush?"

"I don't want to be old for my children."

"Maybe you won't find someone before you're thirty. I didn't. Of course my criteria is different from yours. It's not about kids. I won't marry anyone I wouldn't look for in the afterlife. In paradise, if there is one. If it's just about the here-and-now there's no point getting married."

"You don't believe in the afterlife," Harry retorts.

"I never said that."

"You did. You said things happen for no reason. No reason means no God."

"I guess I'm not as careful a thinker as you are. The afterlife I imagine is a wet field on a foggy day. Whoever put that field in my imagination isn't particularly interested in symbolism."

"You're here for a good time, not a long time."

"If your purpose in life is to be entertained, people over thirty are the enemy."

At the gangway, Harry holds up his black-stained hands and says, "Why didn't the guy who read our fortune warn *me* about the waters?"

3. July

"Grizzly Adams is thirty-five. Anyone over thirty-three is too old to be Jesus."
—Said during a lunchtime dispute between two punk rockers at the Halifax War Memorial in the Grand Parade.

UPBOUND FROM TROIS Rivières, the brickwork in the starboard Foster-Wheeler tumbles down like a baseless argument. The boiler roars likes something caged.

"Five more minutes. Tops. If we hadn't banked the fires..." the second says to Lucien's watch when they relieve his at eight.

"Then what?" says Harry.

"Kaboom!" With his fingers he splays cartoon vectors.

"It can happen like that?"

"Like that, yes. We'd all be dead. Everyone quartered aft."

For Harry, the issue is existential, not mechanical. His cabin is aft.

The *Douglas* makes Montréal and berths along a wall. Lucien, the second, and the chief shut conduits connecting the two boilers. Air. Water. Steam. The ship stands down. Cooling against hot concrete on a hot night. After two hours, Lucien tries to enter the boiler but it repels him.

"Too much?" says Harry.

"Like the Sahara in the middle of the summer plus ten degrees. If we can drop the temperature some, we'll go in."

"You'll go in," the chief corrects him. He is a stubby man. Broken capillaries map his nose and cheeks. "I want this done right." A compliment from someone not given to them. At seventy-two, having grown up to be the boss, the chief occasionally engages in acts of charity but never compromise.

"Go fetch a pitcher of water with ice from the galley," Lucien instructs Harry. "And tell the cook to fill every ice tray he can find and to put a gallon or so of water in the freezer."

By the time Harry returns, Lucien has made another attempt to enter the boiler and returned red-faced and wincing. "It's my freaking ears," he says. "It feels like they'll combust. Go to the rag bin and get me something to wrap around my head. Cotton, not polyester."

Lucien ties Harry's cotton rags loosely around his ears.

"Do you want me to soak them in water for you?"

"Definitely not."

He drinks the first pitcher in one draught.

"Okay. Here I go. Do I look like Lawrence of Arabia?"

"You've drunk enough to be his camel."

Harry refills the water pitcher four times as Lucien enters through a manhole in the back and re-emerges from the boiler after five or fifteen minutes—however long he can handle the heat. The burners removed from the front, two apertures allow Lucien to be interviewed by Jon, the eight-to-twelve oiler, who engages him with mundane questions that require factual responses.

"Who won the World Series?"

"Don't watch baseball."

"Who won the Stanley Cup?"

"Islanders. Swept Vancouver."

"Good."

"Mike Bossy was MVP."

"Okay."

"Scored the winning goal."

"Did he? You know my father met Stan Makita. He was in the hospital in St. Catharines and Makita was in the next bed. He was a real nice guy. Even autographed a…"

"Jon. Please. Too much."

When Lucien's answers lose coherence or become as vague as a political promise, Jon calls, "Time." Or he leaves when the rags around his head become soaked in sweat and the heat of his own fluids bites into his ears like an enraged animal. He stands then under a fan, arriving at a cool coherence, husbanding his endurance. Re-entering the boiler, he Zens on one aspect of the work.

Mortar on brick.

New brick on mortared brick.

Trowel in mortar.

Mortar on brick.

"What city are we in?"

"Montréal. Near the Irish section—what used to be Griffintown."

"What city are we supposed to be in?"

"Your question doesn't make sense. The contract's for Sarnia but we wouldn't be there for two days."

"That's what I meant."

New brick on mortared brick.

Trowel on mortar.

This hurts.

"Name any movie that won an Oscar for best picture."

"Didn't expect that. Give me a sec."

"Time."

"Not fair. You didn't give me any time. *Around the World in Eighty Days.*"

"Time."

"It won!"

"David Niven? Are you kidding? That film was a piece of..."

"It won."

Mortar on brick.

New brick on mortared brick.

"Did you hear me? I said, what's your name?"

"Lucien."

"What's mine?"

"Your what?"

The work takes three hours during which Lucien loses weight through his arms, the sweat pouring in constant rivulets. To wipe his face is to salt his eyes. His second trip out of the boiler he becomes aware of a curious congregation. The engine room is filling with spectators. The fourth engineer and 8-12 oiler have come down to watch as have the cook and the Lurker. Every exit from the boiler, more people arrive—deck crew who would never deign to enter the engine room: deckhands, a wheelsman, and the second mate. With every re-emergence they applaud. They slap his back. They shake their heads.

When he is done, he slumps in a chair Harry has placed under the fan. The accolades continue; the chief says, "You don't look like much, but you're tough."

Later, in the shower, Lucien realizes he hasn't thought about Olivia during the repair. The longest he's gone in days. He no longer plays the tape.

How to respond?

The passage of news through the *Douglas Canada* follows a meandering course, from the wheelhouse to the galley, where it is relayed to the rest of the crew as lunch or supper gossip, arriving at last to the engine room duly embellished. Lucien gets word of a change in contract the next day while ashore in Montréal. He is drinking in a bar on the refinery strip that goes by two names. The sign above the building reads *George V*. To sailors, it is "The Industrial"—a long, narrow room smelling from entrance to kitchen like a beer-soaked rag. The walls are bordered with life preservers lifted from ships that run regular contracts moving oil back and forth between the refinery docks. They ring the room like taxidermied stags. The sickly sweet wet-rag odour is everywhere except the washroom, with its low trough for a urinal and its numbingly fierce smell of bleach.

Most of that afternoon, Lucien and Harry sit near a man who sits by himself at the bar. He looks grey and wiped out. They watch him polish off a hamburger plate, use the washroom, down a couple draughts, and leave. The entire time his hardhat remains sloped back on his head like it's riveted there—he doesn't take it off to use the john. The hat is yellow and smudged with oil in a way that indicates he's taken pains to clean it to no avail.

Jon is ashore with them and losing money at pool against a local who is preternaturally good, making impossible bank shots. Jon is ex-navy. He was kicked out on drug charges, his tattoos used as evidence against him in a naval court. He keeps raising the bet. Keeps losing. On occasion, someone interrupts their game. "*Je m'excuse,*" the man tells Jon, heads briefly to his table, and returns with a small, cellophaned packet. When he is up playing pool, no one approaches his unoccupied table with its untouched beer.

Other crew members drift in and out according to their work schedules. The bosun, a notoriously quick drunk, arrives at mid-afternoon and by six is talking poetry with the Lurker.

"You can't publish poetry that rhymes anymore. They'd reject William Shakespeare."

"Good," says the Lurker. He gets up to sit with Lucien and Harry.

"Did you hear the contract's been changed?"

They haven't.

The Lurker's information is partial. "Sarnia's scrapped. We're loading for Texas."

Lucien's shrug says one refinery is as good as another—the architecture as utilitarian, the nearest bar as generic. He is still oppressed by his unwritten response to Olivia. Stares forcefully into a blank piece of paper for clues.

Harry asks, "What does that guy keep picking off the bottom of the table? He's got something taped to it."

Lucien says, "Cocaine." His eyes remain fixed on the empty page.

"He's a drug dealer? That must be depressing. You're constantly surrounded by…" Harry scans the bar, sees Jon throw his cue on the table.

A waitress stops at their table to examine their bottles. Holding the Lurker's half-empty beer to the light, she asks, "More?"

The Lurker deliberates with the judiciousness of someone trying to decide whether or not to cheat on taxes. "Yeah."

The waitress is pretty and young and dressed in the uniform of the bar, a tight black t-shirt and a tight, black leather skirt that makes every step a stutter, like she can't decide if she's forgotten something. Her accent is precipitous and her speech has the halting syntax of words retrieved from memory. Verbal starts-and-stops. "My brother. He is. A sailor like you," she tells Harry. "Every few months. He leave home with his bag. You have one?"

"No, a suitcase," says Harry.

"He's new to sailing," Lucien explains.

"Oh, I see." She smiles broadly. "I hope you like. It."

Her smile doesn't seem to want anything.

A ball of discarded paper, letters Lucien had started and abandoned, lay bunched in the middle of the table like an abstract centrepiece. Before Lucien can intercept him, the Lurker has picked up one of the pages and snorted.

"Luci's pussy-whipped."

He folds his arms and puts on an expression imitative of wisdom augmented by his thick glasses. "I've seen it before. His mind's in Goo-Goo Land. I knew a cook when I sailed on the *English River* who was going to get married on his next relief. All he could talk about was money. Did almost no work for two months and drove everyone crazy with the shitty food.

"You can't be in two places at the same time. You're either at sea or at shore and, let's face it, things go better at sea. If you're here in body, you may as well be here in mind. Kapeesh?"

Lucien stares sullenly at the blank page in his head. How to be honest?

A dispute rattles through the bar like an angry language before stepping out into the street for air. Lucien doesn't notice, doesn't care. He knows his letter at last, four words. He writes them quickly. He's been carrying around a stamped and folded envelope with Olivia's address on it for so long that the crease has almost worn through, and he isn't sure he can still use it. Maybe the postman won't deliver it out of self-respect. He seals the paper in it anyway and brings it back to the *Douglas* to decide, but the letter is forgotten when he learns the ship's next port of call.

For four difficult days, the weather storms and the ship tilts at will. Lucien's advice to Harry is to stay at the point of equilibrium—the waterline rung on the engine room stairs—and to keep looking forward. Instead, Harry keeps his head in the sink. Occasionally he turns on the tap.

3 AM and she hasn't answered her buzzer. There's been plenty of opportunity. He rings one last time. Counts to five.

Then he's on the street, confused by an intermittent shadow thrown by a defective streetlight. The nodding acknowledgement of loss. A car whips past, its open windows emitting laughter, the smell of marijuana. The squeal of a balcony door wrenched open. He turns to a voice from above. Olivia. She is perched on the rail of her balcony, a hand cupped above her eyes to shade the rippling light.

"Lucien? Lucien?"

"Hi Olivia."

"When did you… How? I didn't know. I'm not ready."

"I couldn't tell you. I didn't find out we were coming until we'd left port. I'm sorry. Should I go?"

"Heavens, no! Come up!"

She is waiting in the hall wearing a Roots shirt that barely covers her.

"Oh God," she says. "This is… I had no idea what I would feel. I mean, I had some idea. I mean…shut up. Just shut up."

"Who are you talking to?"

"My brain."

They are face-to-face in her apartment, a bachelor, the bed its most prominent furnishing. She's been woken from her sleep to judge by the disarray of the blanket and sheets, the indent in the pillow.

She works her hands like she's rubbing a hard stain off her fingers.

She says, "I finished your book."

"My book?"

"He dies. The ambassador. Of course we infer that from the beginning…"

"Olivia?"

"You read such important books."

"Olivia?"

"Yes?"

"It's been a very long time. We should kiss."

Before he can make good on his words, she leans into him, tilts his head slightly with her hands, up to the side to negotiate his nose. Kisses gently, touchingly. The softness of her lips is impossible after everything that has bruised him over the past two months. He pulls her closer and kisses her hard.

"To hell with gentility," she laughs, "I want you."

"I have to be back in time for watch."

"When's that?"

"Eight."

"O'clock?"

"Olivia, are you awake?"

"No!" She keeps laughing, pleasant at her own confusion. She pulls her shirt off and throws it on the floor. "Five hours. Okay. Let's fuck."

It is the first time he has heard her swear.

The gnat bite of embarrassment, the decorum of undressing. He starts with his shirt, undoes the top button and wrestles it over his head. What next? No man looks debonair hopping on one foot pulling off a sock. He goes at them next. Leans against the wall to avoid complications. Unzips his jeans, pushes them and his underwear to his ankles and steps out of them, nearly tripping as he does.

She watches with an expression of victorious capitulation.

He has never seen a brown woman naked—only part of one in a picture taped to the bulkhead in Jack's cabin. His eyes touch softly and slowly from her face down her neck. She feels him look. Watches him follow the vee of a slender, gold chain to her sternum. Sees him stiffen at the fullness of her breasts, her erect dark nipples. He stops midriff. He can hear her breathing.

The act of facing each other, staring openly, holds them in its impiety.

He says, "Your necklace. Take it off."

Keeping her eyes on him, she feels for the clasp. "Why?"

"I want you more naked than you have ever been with any other man."

"There's only been one."

"Oh."

"Why? How many women have you had?"

"A few."

Then they are rolling together on her bed. She grips between his legs, pulls him into her, and says, "Oh fuck." Then they are grabbing and angling while kissing frantically, breathlessly, as though kissing under water. Then he's pushing her forcefully into the mattress, his thrusts driving her up the bed. She moans freely, pulls him with one hand, the other inextricably tangled in her necklace.

Her head beats rhythmically against the wall. A Humboldt milkmaid kneeling on the bedside table with a hand-painted expression of virtuous profligacy rocks vigorously in time to his thrusts. Catching sight of it, he reaches to prevent it from vibrating off the edge.

"What are you doing?" she says.

"Your thingy's going to fall. I'll put it on the floor."

"Leave it!" She gasps.

"But…"

"Leave it!"

The doll hits the floor and breaks.

At the sound of cracked porcelain, she is lost. She thrashes with one hand and tries to free the other, which is handcuffed in the gold necklace. She tugs uselessly, feels herself letting go and he feels her too. Feels the shudder running through her speechlessly hard.

When she finds her voice she says, "Wow. Jane Austen could learn *a lot* from us."

For half an hour they hold each other. Smell each other. The white line on her ankle, no longer than a fingernail, is from skating when she was six. "No tattoos," she observes of him. His arms are cut and bruised. He has a welding burn on his leg made in combination from the arc of the electrode and too-short coveralls riding up his leg. His hands are mapped with a network of dirt roads. He scrubbed for an hour as the ship was steaming to port, but the black held tenaciously.

When she gets up for water he admires her naked form, the straight line of her shoulders, the curve of her ass. She stands by the running tap waiting for the water to cool, her dark skin flawless, her posture, patrician.

She comes back to bed and holds his face.

"I never knew I could miss anyone this much. Your letters killed me. Why did you stop writing?"

He takes the glass from the bed stand, places it carefully on the floor, pushes her on her stomach, and enters her from behind, feeling her ass, wet with him, pressing against his stomach. Hears her muffled voice in the pillow. "Oh fuck, oh fuck, oh fuck…" The feel of her body convulsively gripping.

Shore leave expires at eight. She walks him to a taxi stand on Barrington, a blue and red flowered possibility in her clubbing sundress. The morning has dropped a cloud and Spring Garden is slick with rain. They hold hands, guiding each other around puddles, Lucien wondering what it was he had to do—something he had promised himself. His mind is exhausted from work and sex, distracted by hunger, defeated by lack of sleep and the overpowering intimacy of smell, by beauty without geometry.

Olivia says, "I hope we haven't made a mistake. I didn't expect you."

"I couldn't tell you. I didn't know where we were going until the *Douglas* left the dock."

"No. I understand. I don't blame you. Even though you had the luxurious pleasure of anticipation."

"The life of a sailor is like the sea itself: predictably dull. It's a life of deflation. Nothing lives up to the anticipation of it. I wouldn't let myself anticipate. Too risky."

"I'm lousy with disappointment. Is it time to tell me about your exes?"

"Promise not to break up with me?"

"Promise."

"What do you want to know?"

"Let's start at the start. How old were you when you first did it?"

"Didn't I already tell you?"

"No."

"I thought I did."

"You didn't."

"The married woman? We were both drunk. She assured me it didn't matter. It was just sex. It was like a mantra for her. She must have said, 'It doesn't matter' a half dozen times while we were doing it in the alley outside a Duluth bar. Have you been to Duluth? Never mind. It's filled with sailors. That was her word for me: 'sailor.' 'Let's do it sailor.' 'It doesn't matter sailor.' 'Deeper sailor.' Like I was expected to role play myself. That was my first experience of the Casanova lifestyle."

"I'm glad for my sake that you sailored on. How many women have you had?"

From a stand outside Maritime Mall they grab the front car and cab to Eastern Passage.

"I don't know what to make of this," she tells him at the gangway. "I feel so…I don't know. Maybe there needs to be a new word."

"If you're going to start quoting *Annie Hall*, I'm out of here. Oh! Take this. Almost forgot." He pulls several twenties from his pocket.

"I don't need your money."

"It's for me. Buy an answering machine."

She kisses his forehead.

"Pussy-whipped," says a voice from the pipe shop.

No one in the engine room moves like Harry, walking like a stoner in a high school hallway, rarely looking where he's going—his interest in peripheries. Coveralls line the top rail of the engine room. Set out to dry they run the gamut of colours, blue, orange, green, grey; some stitched with the names of shipping companies: Upper Lakes, CSL, Algoma, Misener. Harry rifles through their pockets.

It was the 4-8 oiler who suggested the problem. Lucien, Harry, and Jon met him mumbling up the stairs on their way down to start watch. An X bruised into his forehead. "Bloody bolt. Fell on my head." He pointed to the overhead. "Must have come from the winch."

Turning over the watch, the second showed Lucien the bolt. "Sheared. See. That's what happens after forty years of vibration on a million effing bolts. Harry, go up top and look for the other half of a 5/8th bolt. Could be something that blacks us out going full ahead in the Thousand Islands. Can you imagine? Us come crashing into someone's living room to watch TV with them, eh?"

"I expect you'll find it on a pipe or on the mounting bolts of one of the separator tanks adjacent to the cofferdam."

He did look. Made a cursory visual inspection, before the coveralls engaged him.

"What's he doing?" says the second. "Frisking the clothes? Is he arresting them?"

Lucien rubs his chin. "So it would appear."

"Is there anything he doesn't screw up?"

"He's a good kid."

Harry returns empty-handed. The second says, "Jesus, Joseph, and Mary. What in the name of Herbert Hoover's wife were you up to? I sent you to find a sheared bolt not to make friendly with my coveralls."

"I couldn't find it. I thought maybe it came out of someone's pocket."

"Oh." The second rubs his chin. "I guess that makes sense." Then: "You know, Luci, you look about this close to death."

II

Twenty hours after Halifax, the ship staggering south, drunk on the inexplicable motion of the sea.

At the intersection of two currents—one cold, one hot—a deep fog obscures the water. The captain's curve-balling the journey, hooking into the Labrador Current out of respect for the ship's aging boilers. The *Douglas* will be fueling with its own cargo if the turbines muscle against the Gulf Stream, he tells the chief at breakfast, and Lucien, who sits at the next table with his arm crooked around his plate to keep it in check, takes the information out onto a deck swaying like a four-year-old ballerina. Leans against a rail vibrating the frequency of the turbines whirring below. Nothing holds shape beyond the reach of his hand.

The morning before, walking to the taxi stand, he and Olivia had crossed through the Old Burying Ground on Barrington. The clouds were thin and grey, a brief and heavy shower having emptied them of black, the cemetery trees, oaks and chestnuts, still raining in the wind. He'd pointed in passing to a limestone memorial. Grey grown dark with time.

"Major General Robert Ross," he said. "I come here when I feel it's impossible for anyone to accomplish anything important. Ross is the man who burned Washington."

"Is this what you do for pleasure? Walk in graveyards?"

"Sometimes."

"Me too."

He thought but did not say, "It gives one perspective." He was deeply conscious of his desire to not sound dishonest. What it gave, he thought, was the stillness of a moonlit crossing over a silent lake. Something impossible to convey. A quality of warmth. It certainly sounded dishonest.

Whatever she heard, she nodded pleasantly, like she was smiling inside. "What would you say to a child of yours if she asked if there's a hell?"

"I suspect that question," he said to his feet.

"It's serious. I want to know."

There was a speck of parsley on one of her front teeth. He was trying not to look at it.

"I would say hell is a word people use to express their worst horrors and put them out of sight so they don't have to acknowledge the everyday struggles around them. They can live next door to Auschwitz. There's a hotter fire in hell. And I would tell my child that hell happens every day all over the world. And sometimes you can save people from it. But not with prayer."

"What would you say about heaven?"

"Heaven? You'll think I'm crazy."

"No, you're safe. Say anything."

"Heaven is Iceland. Living on the side of a volcano with the Reykjavik harbour for scenery. Complete autonomy from the world you see in advertisements. No fair! You said I was safe. Why are you laughing?"

"I just like you."

He'd read *Journey to the Centre of the Earth* when he was nine. His first "grown-up" book, the adult version of Alice's rabbit hole: a dead volcano leading down, down into the subconscious of history. A child's scouting report on the big world.

"I will take you there."

"Do."

The memories intersect. Halifax and Sorel. Holding hands with Olivia feeling the warmth of her touch in multiples. The man in the Satan's Choice jacket turning more cards, touching them with a scarred finger that looks like it has gone someplace fingers should not go. Drawing into himself.

"You want to go North to the place that isn't. You will go South to the place that is."

If South means Texas, he's got that right. Disturbing.

"You will lose two people, almost three. Help will come from…" Flipping a card crisply. A sitting woman in a regal dress. She holds a scepter, wears a crown. He touches her face with his awful finger, moves to the diaphanous folds bunched in her lap, fingers her like the answer is inscribed in Braille on her crotch. "…a whore. You've dealt yourself a wicked hand." Then, investigating Lucien's eyes, he says, "Stay away from waters. Waters will kill you." His eyes are ocean green and empty.

The recurring dream of the three-year-old: the dream of the ripples.

Little Luci looking out from a fingernail's height above his head into a span of still water reaching forever. Into a world of grey inertia.

A ripple at the end of his vision moving slowly towards him, prodded into action by some secret fear. Silent. Unstoppable. Touching at last against his forehead, just above his eyes.

The sense of touch in a dream.

"Impossible," he thought when he told the story to Olivia, but he could feel it.

"Not impossible," she told him. "*Unheimlich*. Is this why you can't swim?" She was astonished when he confessed it. Of all the absurdities in his life, this is the only one she's called him on. His issue with beauty garnered nothing more than a nod.

Whatever the word, in his memory the sensation is real.

As are the successive ripples coming quick. Time sliding out of its tongue and groove joint. In no time, the dream is a nightmare. The ripples wave. They crash against his forehead, their dull monotony grown insistent by the time a scream forms in his rib cage and pulses at the sight of a hand, just out of reach, slapping the water.

The memory ends in his mother's, arms. Theresa then is Olivia now. The same age. His birth an unseasonable seven months after her marriage. Why does she look so scared, soothing Little Luci back to sleep, reciting melodic e.e. cummings poems in a sing-song voice, promising that everything is safe?

In no time, the ripples return.

Off New England, the ship rolling more perilously than before, like a pendulum bound to no specific rhythm.

On watch, Lucien ties the engine room fridge with its single carton of milk for the coffee to a bulkhead to stop it from roaming the deck, to stop it from smashing into the turbines or into Harry, who sits with a bucket in his lap in a chair tied to the opposite bulkhead. He returns to his cabin at noon to find his Walkman smashed on the deck, shouts, "Fuck!" at the overhead as he tosses it into a drawer. He is usually more circumspect, more in tune to seaboard gravity, but something about the journey—Halifax?—has thrown off the sea instincts that generally stay with him into his relief. When he gets home he'll unpack with a mind for stability, shoring clothes against the potential pitch of the house. When they first started together Sylvia would laugh when, the first few meals at home and in restaurants, he pushed condiments to the centre of the table to give himself time to react to shifts in gravity.

The next day the waters are still, yesterday's tempest, a seeming clerical error, the ocean blue-getting-bluer. The horizon is boundlessly empty: no ships, no shore, no clouds.

From stem to stern, finger length bodies asphyxiate on the hot steel, flying fish. The deck is alive with their grotesque struggle. He picks one up and holds it to his nose, throws it back, doesn't notice he's being watched until the third mate says, "You can't save them all. They'd hop another ship anyway. Nice bit of Darwinian mismanagement. Evolution hasn't taken us into account."

The mate is a short, thick, balding man whose solitary fashion statement, John Lennon glasses, are a curious fit with his bulbous nose, making him look like an accountant. Likely he's invisible on shore. His is an invisible look. On the *Douglas* he sleeps behind a locked door—the only crewmember to do so. No one knows what he fears, so the galley is rife with rumours.

Harry emerges from the after house with a sausage in one hand, a cup of coffee in the other. The bosun follows with a grapefruit and a copy of *The Atlantic*. The bosun is a lapsed chess master, who played professionally before becoming a sailor. Nights when they play chess, Lucien arrives with a bottle of gin. The bosun, an exceptionally easy drunk, marvels that he can never beat Lucien.

Harry rubs his hair sleepily, yawns, and says, "Where are we?"

"South of the Carolinas," answers the mate.

Harry scans the absence of horizon, looks out into a blue that must be two blues meeting somewhere, and says, "Creepy." He bites into the sausage. "This is a different kind of alone."

The mate spanks the rail. "Are you studying to be an engineer or a poet?"

The bosun says, "Speaking of poets, there's this Shelley bit that I think speaks to what Harry feels: *A grief without a pang, void, dark, and drear and…*

drowsy, unimpassioned grief, in its…starless lake of blue." He bites into his grapefruit and everyone else grimaces.

Folding his arms on his chest, the mate says, "Yeah." He kicks a fish. "That's what I was going to say."

Rounding Florida, the heat-held days transform the engine room into a shuddering crematorium. Harry spends whole watches with his head pushed up a fan duct. Jon, whose shirt caught fire when he was five and he misplayed with matches, chafes at the skin grafts peeking out of his collar. Lucien reminds himself not to work. The risk of passing out is too great. Spend the watch watching.

Suppers are gross. He can't keep the sweat out of his food. But the waters are calm, the colours as they steam into the Gulf, paradisiacal. The ships now appearing regularly on the horizon are giants. Texaco supertankers dwarf the *Douglas*, making the contract seem surreal. What use has Texas of Canadian oil?

They arrive on the seventh day out to a Port Arthur refinery at the end of a swamp. Are warned by the shore crew to be on watch for alligators. Lucien stays onboard. Off watch, Harry keeps him company playing euchre.

"Don't you want to say you've been to Texas?" Lucien asks him.

"I'm in Texas."

"Doesn't count until you step ashore."

"It does."

"The ship's not a place."

Harry shrugs. "Who do I know in Texas? I'd rather hang out with you."

"You understand that shipboard friendships don't last? They're situation specific. You may never be in Texas again. You should be ashore buying a spoon. Years from now, you'll be able to say over crumpets that you were in Texas."

"The reason our games take so long is because you always talk when it's your turn to deal. Have you noticed that every time you ask me whose deal it is, it's yours?"

Canada-bound the next day, the Chief tells Lucien he's received word from head office that his relief is hired. He'll be on the dock at the next port or maybe in the canal depending on where the contract takes them next.

Time drops off a cliff. Lucien is impatient with simple tasks, hardly speaks with the crew. Over three years working together he's developed a work-rhythm with Jon, who recognizes the signs of his abandonment when he sees Lucien staring blankly at the control console, a bank of twenty-three sightless brass gauges staring back.

"You've got it something terrible," he says. "Channel fever. I doubt I've seen it so bad."

"I know."

"Don't worry about the watch. You just do what you're doing."

"Thanks."

Steaming past New England Lucien stops speaking on watch. He's silent in the galley and the rec room. At the mouth of the St. Lawrence Jon has had enough.

"You're killing me. I don't care what—say something. What are you thinking about?"

"I'm thinking about the Halifax Explosion. Do you know about that? It was 1917, the end of the First World War was in sight, and two ships collided in the harbour, wiping out the North End."

"Yeah, I know about it."

"The *Imo* was Norwegian; the *Mont Blanc*, Belgian."

"Okay. That's a start. What are you thinking about that?"

"I'm thinking the crews spoke different languages, but the ships had the same engines, triple expansions, so the engine room crews were saying the same things just with different sounding words. They were having the same day. Before the ships blew up."

"Okay. That's good," says Jon, "Do you want a coffee?"

"I don't know."

"Fuck."

And then, one night, the Lurker shakes him from his bed.

"Your relief's at the lock."

"Which lock?"

"St. Lambert."

Montréal. Right.

"Did you sleep in your clothes?"

He did. He recalls wearing them to bed on the possibility he'd pay off either at Côte Sainte Catherine or the St Lambert Lock. His packed duffel bag stands watch at the door like a fully armed lawn ornament. It was half-full when he caught the *Douglas* but now weighs three-months heavier with its unexpected and mostly needless accumulations.

There is no one in the galley to tell cheerio, bye, ta-ta, ciao. He's practiced them all. Even "Adios Casablanca." He has nothing to say to the new man boarding the ship with his own half-filled duffel bag, a man dressed for the *Pax Britanica* from his handlebar mustache down. He never gets to know his reliefs.

This one looks wary, like most sailors catching a ship for the first time, thinking about too much.

At the gangway, Jack offers his hand and Lucien, after all his practiced good-byes, struggles apologetically with his duffel bag, mumbles, "See you," and sidles away without the worry of touching the hand Jack employs when gazing at the décor in his cabin.

Then he is in Mirabel waiting for his flight, his thoughts ungovernable.

The leaving is always this way, always inadequate to the journey. The arrival will be different.

4. August–September

Who here's afraid of Ronald Reagan? He knows if he invaded we'd vote Democrat.
—Said by the bartender at the *Misty Moon Cabaret* to a wasted American petty officer claiming to be a spy.

LATE MORNING AND she looks like she hasn't slept. Halifax airport is awash in suits. She is dressed in a low-cut purple shirt still starched into shop floor right angles. She has never shown him cleavage. Now she does. She has never been a quisling to fashion so far as he knows. Her pleated jeans are a curious capitulation.

They kiss searchingly.

She says, "You are so, so beautiful."

"Yes," he says.

Then they are holding hands shyly in the back seat of a cab speeding through windswept curtains of rain, racing through equivocating shades of black and grey. The driver's manner is to look back while she speaks, to chaperone. Her topics range from the Falkland's War to the most recent passenger plane crash—this time in Louisiana—to the dearth of good television since the cancellation of the *Muppets*. Periodically one or both of them try to redirect her attention to the road.

She says, "I've driven this a thousand times."

Twenty minutes into what should be a half hour ride, they lurch to the curb. Lucien pays the fare, jerks an overstuffed duffel bag from the trunk, and whispers to Olivia, "That was scarier than anything that's happened to me this past three months."

"No kidding."

They stand leaning into each other in the torrent watching the taxi corner Gottingen. Their clothes drenched, their faces wet.

"Go in?" says Lucien, and Olivia sucks in her breath and says, "Yes! Damn it." Then she laughs, exhausted, relieved, hopeful.

By mutual agreement, Halifax starts in his Black Street apartment. It is her first time inside and Olivia helps push aside boxes and move the couch from the middle of the floor to beneath a bay window. They unpack the kitchen and organize the cupboards, arriving after some debate at a shared sense of order. The dining room table lacks legs. Lucien fetches a Kahlua box that clacks with tools and puts the table together while Olivia grinds beans for the percolator. They drink coffee and talk, both of them baffled by the task at hand, by the need to see each other as real people after five weeks of imaginings. When they finish their coffee, they undress with the timidity of schoolchildren on a dare, all the identities they've imagined about each other, about themselves, secretly watching.

When they touch, it's just them.

They spend the afternoon confident in their nakedness, bumping, caressing in every room as they continue to make the apartment agreeable, assaulting the surrounding randomness until everything is intentional. They shower and dress. The rain, having quit abruptly, is punctuated by a glorious stillness that demands witnessing. They pass through the hydrostone section erected after the explosion.

Olivia points to a two-storey, square, white house, unadorned except for a featureless storm porch, the blue and green houses on either side stiffly identical. Two workers on ladders pry shingles off the white house.

"When I first came to Halifax," she says, "I was surprised to find a wooden city. I assumed that cities were built to be imperishable, but here was a provincial capital always in need of repair. It struck me as stupid. Imagine thinking a town is stupid. For two years I was offended by the thought that I lived in an ugly city. All the houses exactly square as though no one had an opinion. After you left and you wrote those gorgeous letters it occurred to me that Halifax *is* beautiful in the way that a verb can be beautiful. The beauty of these houses is that they are always being replaced plank-by-plank every hundred years or so. It's not the way the city looks, but the way it lives."

She gestures at thin men on ladders pulling at the shingles with pry bars, working aggressively with cigarettes clenched in fixed grimaces, squinting at breaking wood through drifting smoke, humming different tunes: the squeal of ripped cedar, the shriek of nails.

"This doesn't make the brochures," she says.

They continue to the water to read together on the nearest dock, get wet sitting on the driest plank they can trust.

Olivia says, "I want this."

"Me too." Lucien wonders, as he always does, whether anything ought to be done.

"Can we sustain this?" says Olivia. "No, we can't, but we can make something, can't we? Something that's permanent." She shifts. He's impressed by her concern. "I want you to remember this. Can you? Never forget this feeling. Things will change."

The light is indeterminate for the departing storm. The horizon looks strange and delicate. The taller waves coolly varnish his toes.

"They have," he says.

They're home at dusk, eat late. He proves he's an indifferent cook with a pot of gluey spaghetti. They eat on the couch out of the pot, legs linked together.

When she says, "I'll never make it as a homemaker," he gets up, takes the empty pot to the kitchen, and returns with a rolling pin.

"I bought this because it's something people have. I'll die never having used it."

She says. "We should try to stay together."

"Try? I'm keeping you. I've decided."

"This isn't just you. We don't know each other."

"We do."

She looks like she's formulating something to say but says nothing.

He wakes up that night to find her looking at him.

"Do you think there's a karma-function that punishes people for being happy?"

"Is something happening?"

"Answer my question." Her expression is ice cream and vinegar.

"No. And if there is, I don't care. I refuse to be punished. If something's happening, you have to tell me."

"Soon. Yes. I have to tell you another story about me...when we're ready."

In the morning, after stepping out to the store for as many perishables as he can carry, he fesses up about Harry. Lucien hadn't expected to be so stupid with a friend. Harry would be back in class before he returned from his relief. The night before Lucien paid off ship's articles, Harry approached him with a scrap of paper, asking for his mailing address, saying he wanted to keep in touch.

"I'll write to you in Halifax. This is my address."

He might have said nothing. Surely, he could have accepted Harry's address and surrendered his and let Harry write the two or three letters he'd write before giving up.

He tells Olivia what he said instead, marveling at his gracelessness. "I told him that it doesn't work that way. You don't get to keep the friends you make at sea."

"What did he say?"

"Not much, just goodbye," he'd broken Harry's confidence so thoroughly.

Harry turned quickly, not before Lucien held out his hand, although he might not have seen it.

"Yes," says Olivia in a voice that means, *I knew that about you.*

That night she says she wants to sleep in her own apartment.

"Will I sleep there, too?"

"No. I just need to be alone. I need to think. I love you. Don't believe for a quarter of a second that I don't."

They start from his apartment the next morning. The weather is drizzle and sun. She arrives exhausted—she hadn't slept—brings coffee and croissants. They add peanut butter sandwiches and apples to their supplies. They walk down Robie, eating as they go. Cutting through a construction site, she limps over loose gravel.

"Are you hurt?"

"Stone in my shoe."

"Do you want to stop? You can lean on me."

"No. I want to pretend it isn't there. It will be instructive."

They hook west around the Citadel and sit to read on a concrete bench on a hill in Holy Cross Cemetery, surrounded by white stones in tightly layered lines. The arrangement brings to Lucien's mind cold waves rushing a steeply slanted shore. Olivia preoccupies herself with incised dates. He opens his book. Tries to read at a speed that will keep the pages from getting too damp from the misty grey while she walks, counts, mutters, "Another." Then: "Another."

On her return she reports, "Nine in this row alone."

He looks up from his novel.

"Nine?"

"Women who died in their late teens to early twenties." She drops onto the bench, takes off her shoe and shakes out a large pebble.

He can't suppress his alarm. Her karma-function. The gravestones. "Can I ask you a personal question?"

"Yes."

"Are you pregnant?"

"Now there's a question. I missed my period. It's probably nothing. My cousin Maud, who's an expert on all things concerning sex, says it's not real. I hadn't had sex in years. I didn't want anyone before you pissed me off. It's to be expected that my body is wonky. It's nothing."

"You taking this to Maud means it is *something*."

"Because I'm afraid of her? She was surprisingly kind by which I mean she was clear and efficient. Efficiency is kindness when you're facing disaster. She said she'd take care of me."

"Family is important. I'd like to meet her."

"She'd like to meet you. She says she knows all about sailors. She's hoping you're different. I'm surprised what a relief this is. I worried...because I didn't tell you right away. I don't know. Should have. Couldn't. I needed a day or two to be sure you and I were real. Please don't be angry. It seemed so impossible."

"If you are pregnant, I'm not leaving you. Not unless you tell me to."

"Lucien, getting knocked up is no basis for a permanent relationship, and that's what you're talking about. We don't live in Alabama."

"No."

"I do want you. I know that for certain. I love you. That's a fact, too. You may be the first man I've met who's honest. I don't know why you're honest. It's probably a fault. I mean, you broke with Harry. But the reason I've been single for three years isn't just because of this." She holds up her hand. "No ring will ever fit on this finger, but that's not what we're talking about. The reason I haven't seen anyone is because until you there's been no one else who I can imagine myself holding hands with in Iceland or any other impossible place. To be honest, you're not even the best looking man to try to win me. I put you at number three. I was in class last term with this guy with super broad shoulders. I always sat behind him. Never mind. Not the right time for jokes. I want to go home and I want to do you and I want neither one of us to make any decisions based on the fact that we're afraid. We love each other. I could be pregnant. Those are two facts.

"And maybe not every disaster is a disaster. My love for you is so, so great. I could hardly sleep when you were gone. I wanted you so bad. Just to be with you. I learned that again last night."

Afterwards, when they lay wrapped in each other, she cups his face in her hands and says, "You are so, so awkward."

He marvels at his lack of fear.

The next morning, wandering downtown holding hands. Olivia says, "Is that your..."

A ship lies at anchor. A red postage stamp enveloped in grey and black buildings—a trick of contours and Prince Street appears to terminate on its deck.

"Yeah. Must be waiting to load."

They continue to the water, find a patch of quiet to consider the *Douglas* where the harbour smell is tolerably septic.

"How do you feel?" she asks.

"I don't know. It's not one thing. Work isn't supposed to visit me on vacation. I feel in part like I've been invaded." He tosses a stone at the ship that plops into the water a half kilometre short of its target. "I'm more worried about what I don't feel."

"What's not to feel?"

"Friendship. Almost every one of my friends is on that ship."

"I want to meet them."

"I don't know if that's a good idea. We're not like you."

"You keep believing that about yourself but it's not true. You're not two people. You're one person doing two things."

"If you think so."

"This is important."

"Okay. We'll wait for them to come to us."

"How?"

"I'll show you."

They wander south until the crowd is nothing, the smell less invasive. They settle on two reasonably smooth rocks out of way of the spray of waves and sit reading. Periodically, Lucien assesses the *Douglas*, his eyes tracking from stern to bow. They've been at their watch the better part of two hours when he rises, brushes the seat of his pants, opens his bag and exchanges his book for an apple.

"What's happening?"

"There." Above the *Douglas*, a thin line of black smoke hangs from the base of a larger ball like a string tied to a coughed-up balloon. "They're making demands on the boilers. Time to go."

He takes her to a converted *Walmart* on Prince that is now a bar called *Wally's*. The renovations have been slight. The shelving units are gone, but not the ceiling tiles or the industrial lights. The vinyl floor is the same. Two bartenders slouch over a slightly off-keel table by the door. They treat Olivia to a careful indifference that tells her she's an oddity. Lucien orders two pitchers. The more energetic of the two gets up slowly and pours.

They choose a long table, a darkly-stained wooden board for twenty, away from the bar near two scuffed-up pool tables. The selection on the jukebox doesn't know the eighties—it hardly knows the seventies. Lucien empties his pockets of quarters and they sit listening to apocalyptic Summer of Love music of the *Surrealistic Pillow* variety.

"What if they don't show?"

"They will. In every port a sailor can get into a cab and say, 'Take me to the zoo,' and the driver will take him *somewhere*. That's a night trip. In the afternoon, 'Take me to the sailors' bar'—in Halifax—brings you to *Wally's*. Don't worry about them not showing. I've seen them here before. If you want, we can walk up to the zoo with them later. If you want to see the true meaning of sailing."

The men at the bar consider Lucien, whisper, stare openly at Olivia.

"You go without me. Meeting your friends here will be enough."

"Afraid of what you'll discover?"

"Of being discovered."

Afternoon regulars, men who would be voiceless anywhere else, arrive and crowd the counter. A woman in a pink tank top and pigtails, young and passingly sexy, enters and takes up a defensive position at the end of the bar. What table service she offers she dispenses with cool indifference to anyone sitting outside the compass of a ten-step walk from her station: her language that of a fifteen-year-old sneaking a cigarette at recess. "Ain't that the way," or "No kidding," or "Yeah, fuckers," she says in reply to a litany of jeremiads from stooped men with time-creviced faces, who've spent their mornings wandering.

"Nice place," Olivia observes.

One pitcher is warm, the other empty, by the time the crew of the *Douglas* settle in, Jon and Harry in the first wave. They start at the sight of Lucien.

"Oh ho!" says Jon. "Couldn't stay away from the ship?"

"I'm not the prodigal. The ship is. It couldn't stay away from me. I'm just holding its table."

"Hi," says Harry. "You must be…"

"This pitcher's for share?" says Jon.

"*Mais oui.*"

"Olivia. And you're Harry, Lucien's best friend. It's good to meet you."

"Me and the engines have heard a lot about you."

"I knew I was going to like you," she says. "You're the kind one in his letters, the confidante who keeps him straight."

"Really?"

"If half the things he's said about you are true, you and I are friends."

He smiles a Harry smile.

"And you're Jon."

"All lies. Everything he's said about me. You and I will never be friends."

Olivia laughs. She offers a hand.

"You need to get that fixed," he says.

"It's good to be on an even keel," says Harry. "You wouldn't believe that last trip. Couldn't eat."

"That rough?"

"New cook," says Jon. "Never worked in a kitchen."

"How'd he get hired?"

"Owner's nephew. Wanted summer spending money. The intricacies of frying eggs are beyond him. Speaking of which, your relief's a deadbeat. Could go at any time."

"What? No. It's only been two weeks. Can't they hire someone who can stick it out for a month?"

"No one in the office has ever worked on a ship. Everyone they hire is a loser. They wouldn't know the difference between a farmer and a sailor if... Complains about everything. Thinks you left him a disaster, which is really a complaint against me. As I recall you did no work the last week before you left."

"Sorry."

"Don't be. I know how it is. I intend to do no work when you come back. But, Jesus, this guy tightens a bolt and he writes it up in the logbook for posterity. The chief keeps telling him to stop, but he says it's in his union contract to leave his signature on anything he touches. Someday someone might read the log and he wants everyone to know on such-and-such a day at such-and-such an hour he cleaned a filter or *Brasso*ed the telegraph."

"Are engineers that vain?" says Olivia.

"Yes," they reply in unison.

There are four pitchers at the table now. Olivia is losing at pool to a solicitous Jon. The bosun, Jack, and the Lurker, wade through a now-packed room to their table. The bosun drops into Olivia's chair and shakes his head. Seeing Lucien beside him, he says, "Jesus, what are you doing here?"

"I hate that question."

"Look. Playing pool. A girl," says Jack. "Last place I'd expect to find one of those."

"She belongs to Luci," says Jon. "Her name's Olivia."

"Pussy-whipper," says the Lurker.

Olivia looks up from a shot she's angling, calculating with a philosophy-major's eye vectors she won't make. She blows the Lurker a kiss, which he grabs in the air and rubs against his crotch.

The bosun says, "Don't mind him. He just saw his life flash before his eyes. I'm sure he's feeling disappointed with himself. We got into a bad cab. Bad driver. Stoned out his brain."

"If he has one," says the Lurker.

"Kept trying to push us the speed he was on," adds Jack. "We said we weren't buying any of it, so what does he do? Tries to sell us his car."

"I told him we were on a ship," says the bosun. "What would we do with your fucking car? And he says, *it's a good car. It's green.*"

Olivia claps. "Please keep talking."

"Oh, that's nothing," says Jon. "I once got into a cab with the man who didn't blow up the Jacques Cartier Bridge."

"Oh yeah, I remember," says Jack. "Tell that one."

"Me too," says the bosun.

Jon says, "It was last Spring. I get into a cab in Montréal and the driver says, *I'm the man who didn't blow up the Cartier Bridge.* So I tell him, *We're on the Cartier Bridge,* and he says that's because it didn't blow up. He put a bomb underneath it but it wasn't a real bomb. It was a real-looking bomb. He said it was made of toilet paper rolls and wires."

"We were there, the Lurker and me. Tell them, Jon."

"No, you weren't there. You've heard me tell this before. I was the only one in the car. Can I get on with this? So I say to this guy, *What's the point of planting a toilet paper bomb?* and he says, *I called the police and they traced the call and I went to jail.* And he drove like he talked. The same attention to detail. Like someone who'd gone to jail for planting a fake bomb and calling the police on himself. Here's the other part of the story. Shore leave had expired and, before I knew the guy was crazy, I said I'd tip twenty bucks if he got me to the ship before she sailed. I didn't know he'd just gotten out of jail and was committed to his job. Passed a cop on a narrow street doing double the speed limit. I think the cop was too shocked to turn on his siren."

"Okay," says Jon, "now top that."

"I have one," says Lucien, "but it's just bad. There's no way of spinning it into a joke."

"But don't you have any sailing stories?" says Olivia.

"Those are sailing stories!" The bosun sounds affronted.

"No, something that could only happen on a ship."

"Oh, I see what you mean. You want a storm. Okay."

The table falls silent, everyone running through his inventory of encounters at sea with the weather. The bosun speaks first: "I was in a really bad one years ago when I caught my first ship. Superior storms are worse in my experience."

The Lurker and Jon say, "Yeah." Jack says, "Don't be crazy. The ocean is worse than any lake."

The bosun continues: "There was a waterspout moving across it and ships were putting into port. We knew that, but our captain was Captain Crunch."

"Like the cereal?"

"Old sailors' joke. Sooner or later every captain gets that nickname. But this one deserved it. He should never have put us past Whitefish Bay. And the ship was a real bucket, the *Saskadoc*, built for the seaway before the expansion. Maybe 425 or 450 feet. A package freighter. We were running light on ballast to Thunder Bay, so high in the water. And the storm hit us straight on and the waves were fists pounding away at the hull, trying to push us over. Five minutes into it even the captain's afraid, which was good. I was the wheelsman for the worst part of that storm, and the mate wanted me to turn the ship back for Whitefish, but the captain wouldn't have it. He knew if we turned against the waves we'd capsize sure as shit. Those waves were over thirty feet. We come up one and crash down, the deck invisible for the wash. Steered straight into it is what we did. Made no forward progress the whole night. The waves kept hammering us back. At the end of six hours we were a half hour behind where we'd started. But still afloat."

"I would have been terrified," says Olivia.

"So the end of it all is, we ride it out and make Thunder Bay in the morning. If we'd waited out the storm we would have arrived as soon. In the sixteen years since, I've never been through anything that terrible. When we made the elevator and docked, I stood on the bow and looked back to the stern and the deck was curved. The waves had bent the fucking superstructure! Like this." He twists his arm. "Like the ship was in need of a giant vice to get hammered straight again." He nods at Harry. "I had a bucket by the wheel that kept tipping over. It wasn't just me. The whole bridge was awash with vomit. It was on our hands, on our clothes. Now is that what you call a sailing story?"

"Yes," says Olivia. "That's a sailing story."

"I've got one."

"Me too."

One by one the crewmembers tell tales about the first time they vomited at sea. During a particularly grotesque story, Lucien observes Olivia slide her novel out of her bag and scribble Harry's address on the title page. He listens to her recite both of their addresses to Harry, who nods, catches Lucien's smile and winks.

"Tell me your story," she says that night. "The cab ride that isn't funny."

"I don't know."

"What's not to know?"

"It's not important except to me. Somebody else might say it was nothing. It happened when I was on the *Soo River Trader*."

"The time you lost your virginity."

"No, I didn't lose that. I threw it away. It isn't always something hard that leaves a mark. A thing turns, and it doesn't turn back. Maybe this only matters because I was eighteen and because I'd just gotten off the farm. Nothing—absolutely nothing—in my childhood prepared me for the life of a sailor. Not my dad's vineyard, not school, not church. When I caught my first ship I had no manual, no tools, no idea how people worked. But on board the *Trader* was this boy, who I imagined was like me because we were the same age. He was a hick like me, and carried himself with the same wide-eyed stupidity, always asking advice and ingratiating himself with the crew because he made them feel like geniuses. Everyone called him Rocky. Even his mother addressed letters to him as Rocky. I was connected to myself through chumminess with him and his astonishing ignorance. I thought we were stupid in the same ways, until we went clubbing in Montréal."

He tells her that he knows the story in a half dozen mental photographs which he describes: 1) Drinking at a posh bar in the early afternoon, sun streaming in the tall windows. 2) Drinking in a dirtier bar beside a night-black window. 3) A cab ride in the dark. 4) A lost argument, Rocky demanding a detour. 5) Lucien staring forward at passing lights trying not to hear a hooker in the backseat working Rocky's cock. "That sort of thing is nowhere near as sexy as it sounds in porn. No sexier than the sound of a geriatric choking on a pancake." 6) The woman keeping Rocky on the clock. "She kept saying, 'You've got two minutes and I'm done,' but they were at it long enough for him to get his money's worth."

"How do you know he got his money's worth if you were in the front?"

"She rolled down her window and spat. What I remember most about that night was walking slowly up the gangway. I can feel the steps. I might have turned around and gone back to a goodly Christian farm. Christ knows, I wanted out. I kept going, went in. A friend of mine was in a bad accident on that ship, and it left him mentally impaired to the point of religious fanaticism. He found his childhood, and I lost mine. I imagine that someday I'll go back to the *Trader* and walk on deck and know who I was before. Then I'll go to Iceland."

She says, "I'll find out Monday. Whatever I learn, I already know what I feel. Fuck, I want to keep you." She says, "I wouldn't change anything. That's how I know this is good."

II

He's dripping wet from the tub. The voice on the phone belongs to Sylvia. Olivia watches from the couch.

"How did you know I was in town?"

"Cathy told me."

"Cathy?"

"No one walks like you. You're easy to spot. I'm calling to invite you out on a non-date. A bunch of us are going for a drink tomorrow night. I want you to come. Just as friends."

"I can do that."

"Yes." A pause, then: "I know how busy your schedule is."

He stands naked in a puddle of bath water. Olivia stares at his crotch. She takes off her necklace.

At the Tower Street apartment watering plants that afternoon they find a message from Sylvia on Olivia's machine inviting her too.

"This might be the time for us to go public," she says. "Then I'll be able to answer your phone."

"Let's play it by ear. You have to catch Sylvia in the right mood. My habit when I wanted something she might not like was to start slow. Feel things out."

"It's a simple, declarative statement. We haven't known each other long enough to stretch it further."

"Just see if she's even-keeled. That's all. Remember: we like her."

They meet at Dick Turpin's, Lucien, the last to arrive. He's been kept late by workers ripping up a roof on Tower Road, three men in overalls pulling shingles and dropping them carelessly into a blue bin below. He'd been listening to the peculiar sound of labour, the echoing crash of wood in an empty bin competing with bird songs, traffic, an argument broadcast through an open window down the street, a distant train shunting onto an unseen siding.

Sylvia has saved the chair beside her. Olivia sits across the table between 'maybe Dave' and Cathy. Olivia's, "Hello," is spoken with spy aloofness. Cathy regards her from the epicenter of an unsettlingly simmering calm. Why? He thinks back to Sylvia's phone call: *No one walks like you. You're easy to spot.* Was he walking alone? Maybe not. Already he and Olivia have a lovers' lean. If they're walking, they're holding hands. Rubbing shoulders, looking where each other is looking. Talking with the expressions of people telling stories not giving instructions or expecting catharsis.

Cathy's clipped, "Hi," sounds wrong.

Sylvia is dressed to impress. She wears perfume. She never wears perfume. Her look is *Le Château*—cropped pants, a double V-neck striped jacket. That's not her. She read *The Second Sex* early in their relationship and her style changed from anything current to Simone de Beauvoir in pants. The last time that he can remember her spending money on a complete outfit it was on a sombre black affair. He had been her secret sharer then, the lover who'd sat with her through her grief at her father's funeral. That had bound them in sympathy, gotten them through years of incompatibility. It had left him with a deep, non-sexual love for Sylvia, put him in awe of her emotional strength. Before that it hadn't been a category for him. Beautiful people born into ease weren't supposed to move inward with their sorrow, contain it like a jar of night. They weren't supposed to know how. Sylvia was beautiful. She was safe. She had never known the fear of eviction. Her father, a legal-aid lawyer, was the prime audience of her identity until he died. One day, they went jogging together. She thought he tripped. She could not get him up.

A week after the funeral Lucien held her as she shuddered and cried in her sleep. "It's okay. It's okay," he said. "It's just a dream. It's all gone."

"I dreamt you tripped."

And he was aware of how totalizing the loss had been. How big the jar. He didn't want to be with her, but his need to protect her, to believe the world was good if she were safe, had led him to move back in with her.

She has removed a shoe. She brushes her foot against his leg with the single-mindedness of a neglected cat rubbing against a fencepost, and he wonders what's gone on in her life since he last saw her.

Maybe Dave, who is dressed for golf in Scotland, says, "Hey."

Cathy is wearing the same outfit she wore the time she came to his and Sylvia's apartment. Maybe that doesn't mean anything. What is she thinking? It was only one time, but they should know things about each other. They should like what they know.

"I have an announcement," says Olivia, and he would stop her if he could, but he can't. "Lucien and I are seeing each other."

Sylvia reddens like she's slapping herself from inside. She leans down, forces her shoe back on.

Maybe Dave says, "This calls for a toast. Here's to all sorts of things too corny to say." No one raises a glass.

Olivia's smile shows signs of exhaustion before Cathy says, "That's no big deal. We've all done that."

"Done what?" demands Sylvia.

"Slept with Lucien."

Sylvia knocks over her chair and quits the room without looking back.

Olivia's smile capitulates.

"Really?" says maybe Dave. "How is that possible?"

Cathy looks at him sourly.

"I mean *when*? You don't know each other."

"I'm sure that's something they'll want to discuss," says Cathy.

When they are gone and Olivia's order of ginger ale insures they won't be bothered by the waiter again, there is nothing to be aware of but each other. Lucien says, "It was after the first time we met in this bar. You and I still didn't know each other. We'd only spoken twice."

"Why didn't you tell me?"

"I thought it might not matter. I've seen other people. You've imagined yourself with classmates..."

"It matters. Especially now. Everything is changed. Don't you get that?"

Her eyes look frighteningly aware. Sylvia had sold Olivia as intelligent, had said, "She's the top student in her classes. She doesn't go out much. You'll like her. She has no friends."

And now Sylvia is back, her expression brick-steady.

"I am sorry," she says. "That was wrong. Give me a week to process this. I want to stay friends. I love you both."

When she is gone with her unexpected dignity Olivia says, "There better not be karma in Iceland."

Lucien learns the *Soo River Trader* has been scrapped from a ferry captain named Kyle, a fellow reader with whom he has a drinking relationship. Engineers and captains don't generally mix, but after years of running into each other infrequently in a sailors' bar near the water, they read at the same table, conscious of each other's turned pages, keeping pace with each other's drinking. So long as one of them bends into his book, the other does not speak.

The second day after Olivia's announcement to the group, Captain Kyle greets Lucien on Barrington with, "Your ship has been scrapped. We're shaving with her."

Lucien puzzles over what that means as they continue towards Lower Water side-by-side, keeping a respectful-enough distance to be a nuisance to oncoming pedestrians.

"What ship?"

"The *Trader*. Didn't you say she was your first?"

"Yeah. But that can't be right. I saw it in the canal in June."

"That would have been her last trip. They scrapped her in June."

"But it was *my* ship."

"I've lost half of mine." He shrugs. "And a town."

"How do you lose a town?"

"Mining town. Ran out of things to mine. The place was on wheels. Got shipped down Highway 17 to another hole in the ground."

"I didn't know you were from Ontario."

"Isn't everyone?"

"Do you want to get us beaten up?"

Captain Kyle snorts. They arrive at their bar and he holds the door.

"Coming in?"

"No." Something disqualifies Lucien.

He takes the news to the water. He's been avoiding it, avoiding his usual dock for fear of running into Olivia. It has been two days of the wrong kind of silence. Two days during which he cannot extract his reason from his mood. Even obscured by time, buried beneath a ten-year mountain of memories, the *Soo River Trader* is the ship he dreams in his nightmares, and it is in his nightmares that he is closest to eighteen.

A noontime crowd picks through Historic Properties window-shopping their reflections. He wonders what's happening to Holy James, if he's caught another ship or chucked it in. Become a waiter. James was reborn on the *Trader* in as close to a literal sense as possible. He was young, full of anger and, usually, alcohol when a steel girder in a loose hoist swung free hitting him squarely in the forehead, splitting his hardhat in two. James survived, but the blow knocked him back into his childhood. Who knew that his bullying profligacy was the knee-jerk rebellion of someone too unsteady to take himself seriously? He returned to work several months later decidedly repetitive, stuck like a stylus in the old groove of his church upbringing. The crew accepted him because, even transformed, he was one of them, this impossible figurehead perched on the bow, arms reaching into lightning storms, mouth contorting a bedlam of biblical passages—James' apocalyptic performances soon so commonplace the wheelhouse was no longer creeped.

"The waves begin in heaven," James told him the summer he grew up.

"Do you mean the wind, the moon, or tectonic shifts?"

"All of it."

What Lucien never admitted to anyone on the *Trader* was how eerily close his upbringing had been to James'. You have no choice. If life is a journey, it is a journey in a trolley on a track.

Somewhere a hammer pounds *thack*s into the air. *Thack. Thack. Thack.* The bursts rap sharply off the cul-de-sac, become, in echo, two hammers, one him.

He turns from the water and the past and all things that move for no particular purpose, waves and girders and sex. Heads west then north into a thicket of wood buildings, square quadrates being pried new one plank, one shingle at a time—the *thack*ing always one street over. Lucien allows himself to be led by the sound working like fingers on a Ouija board, directing by mystic vibration or subconscious intent. He looks up to see he's arrived on Tower Road.

The weather is easing after a hot week, touching with a cool wind. She stands behind him. He knows her by the sound of her "Luci?" Her arms are loaded with grocery bags, her eyes red; evidently she's wiped her nose and hasn't made a clean job of it. He is struck as always by her beauty.

"I'm pregnant. That's a reality. I peed on plastic."

"Okay."

He takes her bags.

"I…um…could you say something else?"

"Sorry! I'm terrible at this sort of thing."

"If you're telling me you've consoled a pregnant woman before, I don't want to hear it. I've had a crummy-enough morning."

"No! It's just…" He searches for the appropriate, exact words. "I'm terrible at being good enough for someone like you."

"You'd better be good enough. Me and Baby are keeping you."

They walk towards her apartment.

"I miss you. I can't sleep thinking you don't like me. It's been two days and that's too long. I never want to think we won't be together. Promise me you want me."

"I promise," he says.

At the door to her building she stops and bites her lip in her Olivia-way.

"What do you say we talk about the future? The hard things."

5. September–December

Got any bowls of fruit?
—Said to an artist selling watercolours outside the Public Gardens by a businessman shopping for his office.

THE AIRPORT CROWD is thick the afternoon he flies back to the ship.

"I don't do nostalgia," she says.

"You're the one who packed the peanut butter sandwich."

"That's what I'm thinking. I don't know why I did that."

"Maybe you're afraid of changing your luck."

"You have to keep your promise."

"You won't leave school."

"Your promise to love me. I have to trust you. It's hard. There's a lot against us."

"Like what?"

"My history. Your history."

"You still haven't told me yours."

They sit nestled between two families in a crowded row of chairs.

"I was raped by the neighbour's son when I was sixteen," she begins. "Don't say anything. Let me finish. This isn't going where you think it's going. I'm not looking for sympathy."

The family to their right leaves.

"The guy who raped me was twenty-two and he was good looking in a beach-body Leif Garrett sort of way. Blonde curls. Full lips. Dreamy eyes. He could have been on TV. He got me drunk one night when our parents should have been watching us. He told me later it was my idea. I don't remember doing it, but that's how I lost my virginity. I kept our secret because I was in love.

He wasn't smart but he was funny. He was the furthest thing from worldly but he seemed mature because he worked out at the gym. I didn't know anyone who did that. I was bookish. I'd hardly dated at all and I hadn't dated any guy with a job that paid. Construction. I was in high school but when I was in his apartment I was an adult. He bought me a diamond ring. One of those fifty-dollar strip-mall-jeweler's specials. Probably we wouldn't have gotten engaged if there hadn't been a sale. Putting that ring on my finger was the most important thing I'd ever done. And then he took it off. That's how I got this finger."

"Why?"

"I was too good for him. We would have been okay if he didn't know that. I was fine with it. He was really gorgeous so he was a catch and the way he looked at me when I was naked meant I was beautiful; also he made for an awesome Valley-Girlish rebellion. The bad news was he was just introspective enough to know he couldn't keep me. Sooner or later I was going to get bored. I came to the apartment from school one day and he'd flipped. I don't know what triggered it specifically. Maybe he saw me standing too close to a friend. To be honest I stopped caring about what I might have done and how it might have been my fault when the first blow landed. There's something that turns a girl's stomach about being lectured to on love by a guy who's beating up his girlfriend. He kept saying I didn't respect him and that I was probably seeing someone else. He knocked me down. He stood over me, his feet on either side, pinning my arms."

The family to their left leaves.

"He told me how much he loved me *while* he was kicking me and I could see it was no contradiction. He picked me up. I thought I was free. He just wanted to punch me. I took out the coffee table on the way down. All the while he kept saying this I-love-you shit. Imagine! He's kicking and punching and repeating it *ad nauseum*. I tried to shield myself and the situation took a decisive turn for the worse. He saw the ring."

She looks at her misshapen finger.

"I would have given it to him. He didn't have to yank it off. Jesus, I didn't want to be rid of it, I wanted it to never have been. Nearly killed me—the depression. I was suicidal for months. Just the thought that a living, thinking person would be willing to inflict that much pain on me. Someone I was fucking two or three times a day. You know what high school kids are like. Full of effort."

"What did your parents do?"

"Oh, they were good. They love me. The other kind of love."

"Our kind."

"No. Ours is something else. I don't know what this kind is, I've never been here before." She observes the empty chairs on either side of them with an expression of embarrassment. "Who knows how many kinds there are?"

"I keep forgetting something," Lucien says. "Something that has to be done."

A month later, in Bayonne, New Jersey, and her answering machine no longer picks up. She isn't erasing her messages. Is she listening to them repeatedly? Listening to them at all? The answering machine says with a beep its cassette is full.

The beginning of September and the refinery in Bayonne—the closest tanker dock to the Statue of Liberty—in the grip of a heat wave. Everywhere cracked concrete radiating like the inside of a boiler. He can't sleep. His cabin is impossible. And now her phone is turning him off.

The nearest drink to the refinery a shit-bar the size of a trailer park home, four bar stools, eight chairs grouped round two melamine tables. Maximum sitting capacity is twelve, ten during a fight. The barmaid bruised, sweaty, looks like she doesn't need any more excuses to quit, but can't. He hopes the mark on her arm is a tattoo. When he tips she says, "You forgot this."

"It's yours," he says.

"Okay."

He sips slowly, intending to burn off an hour before his next phone call.

The voice on the phone is unfamiliar.

He says, "Olivia?"

"No, Maud."

"Toronto Maud?"

"That's right, Lucien."

"How is she? Is she there?"

"She's not ready. Um…she says to call back in an hour. Can you make it to a phone then? Will you still be in port?"

An hour later, she picks up.

"Luci, don't be angry. Please, please don't be angry. It wasn't my fault."

"Are you okay? Just tell me that."

"I lost the baby."

A whispered, "Don't say any more."

She's cups the phone. Another voice speaking words too muffled for clarity in a tone of decision.

"I can't talk. Can you call back tomorrow?"

"I'll be at sea."

"Call back when you're next in port."

"That could be a week…"

"Please!"

Five days later, in Montréal, he calls a dozen times.

A letter arrives that month.

> Lucien,
>
> *I can state for the record you are the most important man I have known. It was all so quick and yet no relationship has been so important to me as the one we might have had.*
>
> *I understand you will probably hate me and that makes this letter harder than anything I've written.*
>
> *When I lost the baby, I realized I had moved too quickly. We both did. I cannot get back to where we were when you came back to me that night. If I could be there and feel what I felt when I saw you from the balcony I would stay in that place, that emotion, forever. But I've lost something.*
>
> *When we were having the baby, we became those people, the ones who argued for a week straight. Would I stay in school? Would I finish my degree? You offered stability, but stability isn't what I need. I would have accepted your offer for the sake of the baby but then what? I don't know you.*

"Bull shit! Ricardo Montalban knew his future wife for forty-five minutes when he proposed. They're still together."

> *When you went back to the ship, I cracked. My head couldn't take anymore. I was institutionalized for a week.*
>
> *I know I said we could do this, and it's not your fault that I can't. We don't have to. Let's accept that. I'm not going to say that I love you. After what we've been through it would read like a complaint and you're important. You deserve better than that. Don't look for me. I'm in Toronto. I've decided not to come back.*

There is no postscript.

Lucien reads the letter until the pain settles permanently in his stomach. Then he opens his porthole and throws her words into the Seaway.

For two months he is numb. His numbness starts in his mind, touches into his heart and circulates through his veins.

In December, the ship stops in Halifax for a long refit.

He stands on the dock, his jean jacket tight on a heavy, black sweater fuzzed with age, his white running shoes yellow from oil on deck. He looks out on an icebound city and says, "You're wrong."

II

On a steel cold Monday with the wind howling in his head, Lucien stumbles down a morning sidewalk bustling with people shielding their foreheads against a winter squall. No loitering says the sign at the Legislature, where commemorative canons barnacled with ice point snow at parked Rabbits. Tripping over Barrington, packed clouds fumble snow. He stops on Granville and stamps his feet. Was it real the time he stopped here with Olivia?

"What will we say?" she'd asked that morning, and that morning he couldn't say. September and the ship two weeks away. They had a one thirty doctor's appointment to confirm the news they'd read and reread on a pair of home pregnancy tests. Killing time. They'd found themselves looking beyond their reflections into a store window, flowery, happy pictures giddily festooning a sky blue wall. A sharply-casually-dressed woman behind a shiny desk pretended not to be aware of their gaze. Peered sideways, observed them peripherally, retreated into a clutch of mannerisms: rubbing her ear, bending over the page she wasn't reading, tapping it with a pen.

She looked cubicled.

"Will we go in?"

He sucked in his breath and exhaled a decision. "No." Too risky. Then: "Do you think I'm a coward?"

"On the contrary, I think you're an adventure."

He squeezed her hand, kissed her neck. "I know a problem when I can't describe it."

After the doctor's she'd said, "I don't need you. It's not that. But if you leave me, you'll crush me. Absolutely. I'll do okay in an okay sort of way, but this person I like will be finished. She'll never again think anyone important likes her."

No Olivia today or ever again, but the same woman at her desk on the other side of the glass, looking like spring.

He is winter. His eyes hold the baggage of a month's insomnia-blackness. Cleaning-up for shore, he shaved with cold water. His neck is plague-marked with blood dots. A tight jean jacket does little to conceal the work clothes beneath, coveralls reeking of cooked lube oil.

The inside is as warm as the pictures on the walls, sunny shots of people at play. The woman looks up guardedly as though at a street person who doesn't know his place is the street. She's probably had this conversation before, the one that ends with, "We don't keep money in this office."

He surprises her with, "I need information on travel to Iceland."

She processes the statement.

The totality of his research on Iceland is a book published in 1864 in which the protagonist, Professor Otto Lidenbrock, sails from Copenhagen on the *Valkyrie*—a Danish schooner. The schooner has to be chartered and the voyage lasts the better part of two weeks.

"What day would you like to fly?"

Iceland can be reached at his earliest convenience. For twenty years he'd preferred to keep Iceland remote, exotic, the 1864 Iceland of *Journey to the Centre of the Earth*.

She pulls a thick, blue folder from a shoulder-height shelf, her posture as stiff as the No Stopping sign outside the window. Opening the folder to a page of columns in obituary font, she asks, "What specifically would you like to know?"

"I'm sick."

"Pardon?"

"I look this way because I'm sick."

No response beyond a slight uptick of an eyebrow.

"I'd be grateful if you would photocopy any relevant pages on Iceland travel and accommodations from that catalogue. Do I pay for that?"

He reaches for spare cash and pulls from his pocket a hundred dollar bill. The Xerox is in a back room. She returns with a small, neat stack affixed with a pink paperclip.

"Thank you."

"You're welcome."

He holds out the hundred.

"We don't keep money in this office."

Outside the agency he works a cold finger down the first page, crumples it into a ball when he reads, *Reykjavik Holiday Inn*.

He hasn't stepped on Black Street in three months. The mailbox is crammed with flyers, most of the newsprint jaundiced with age. He fights the paper free, all the while imagining the mailman at his task—perhaps a pulpy, sweaty man— at some point realizing the flyers were not being collected before their expiry date and his efforts were purposeless. But he was undeterred. Lucien imagines him on one foot, pressing with the other, his leg raised impossibly high.

He brings the flyers into the house as an undifferentiated mass and tosses them on the table. The apartment smells like a decomposing frat house. He'd charged Olivia with emptying the garbage on garbage-day-eve and retrieving the perishables from the fridge for her use. She's done neither. The perishables perished, the milk deplorable, bread sporting a pubescent fuzz. Some of the contents of the fridge he flushes, some he stuffs into the trash, tying the bag doubly tight to ensure nothing escapes, before carrying it to the bin at the side of the house.

Back inside, he parses for clues. Has she been back? Impossible to tell, but something seems off, some alien arrangement to the order of bottles on the bathroom sink. Or is it the papers beside the bed? Had there been an order? There's none now.

He grabs a pillow from his bedroom, opens the living room bay window, and drops on the couch. The cold is too much. He limps to the bedroom, pulls the comforter off his bed, and returns. Everything in his vision is well-ordered, the books on his two bookshelves arranged by their publishers' colours: rows of black-spined Penguins, cream-coloured Oxfords, a row of blue-backed Reed's Marine Engineering Series. Lived-in books. White veins snake the spines— tracks of a voracious repeat-reader. In a heavy clay pot beside the shelves, the leafy plant Olivia gave him, now brown, is somehow alive.

A picture on the wall beside the bookshelf is askew. He must have bumped it. It was taken on the farm: his parents dressed for church. They've given him the camera. He's four or five and his mother is his focus, the centre of the frame. His much-taller father has lost half his head to his son's proximity. Both of them smile as for too long, waiting for him to have the courage to click. A sudden for-ever-blur. The distortion that comes of wanting to please, of anxiously pressing too hard. No other picture from his childhood comes this close to the truth.

In his dream Pontius Pilate asks, "What is Beauty?" The answer must be important but the phone interrupts Jesus' response, ending the dream. Pushing himself up, his hand slips between the couch cushions and touches a thin ribbon of cold metal.

"Hello." He dangles Olivia's gold chain. Its removal had been a regular silent ceremony signalling her intent.

It's Cathy and she's ridiculous. "How long have you been in town? Why didn't you call?"

"Why indeed."

"Don't be rude."

"How did you know I was here?"

"For Pete's sake, I almost ran you over on the sidewalk. I didn't realize it was you until I was down the street. I tried to catch up but you were gone— God knows where. There's a lot of bars on Granville."

"What do you want?"

"Aren't we friends?"

Surely it's a trick question. "Ah..."

"You are *so* off-putting. Say you're sorry or I'm not coming over."

For no reason he can think of he says he's sorry. When he's off the phone he says to his atrophied plant, "I don't love you."

Cathy is quick. Before his second cup of coffee, she is at the door dressed like a harp seal: tight white parka, tight white snow pants, furry white gloves.

"Jesus, it stinks in here." She pushes past him. "Close the window."

"I'm trying to get rid of the smell."

"Is your head bleeding?"

He recalls slipping on ice on his walk home, touches above his eye. "I think it's stopped."

"You are so accident prone. How long have you been in town?"

"Cathy?"

"Yes."

"Why are you here?"

"Boy are you... Never mind why I'm here. Since I am, I mean to fix you." She runs a hand through the flyers on the dining room table. "Don't throw this out." She waives an envelope. "To you and Olivia."

She drops beside him on the couch, hand raised above her head. When he leans in to grab the envelope she kisses his nose. He holds the letter to the window's light. The return address is Harry's.

"I don't think I can talk... I don't know what happened. She went to Toronto without saying."

"To Toronto? Why do you think that?"

"She wrote when I was at sea."

"Okay. If that's what she said. Look, Luci, I need to know something. That time we did it, were you seeing her?"

"No."

"Promise?"

"Promise what?"

"Promise me that I rejected you, that it wasn't the other way around."

"You told me we weren't suited."

"I remember. And you started seeing Olivia afterwards? That's a relief."

"I don't understand."

"I might have been jealous. Hard to know—having never been jealous before, I have no source for comparison. Tell me something, how long were you and Olivia dating?"

The math is impossible. Time lived between sea and shore is unaccountable, both compressed and empty.

"I don't really know. We were talking until I left in May, but we weren't seeing each other—the way you mean—for at least another month. Wait, why are you asking?"

"Because I've changed my mind."

"About what?"

"I think we're both too emotionally stunted not to be suited."

"Stop playing. This is important! Do you know where I can get Olivia's Toronto address?"

"I know you can't get it from Sylvia. Not after what I said at Dick Turpin's. Sorry. You shouldn't have looked like you were trying to pull one over on me. Now get naked."

"Cathy…"

"Shut up. How sick are you? You're obviously not thinking clearly. You and I are allowed to be naked together if we want to be. It's called the principle of body rights. We've done it and doing it isn't something you can undo. You can't unfuck. You can't unknow. So it's not cheating, if you're worried about cheating on someone who broke up with you. It's okay. Let's just try being tender. Under no conditions are we going to do it unless we want to."

She undresses him, he acquiesces, but he doesn't know why. There's something curiously unsexy about the act. Cathy is deliberate, like she's searching a battlefield touchingly for a wound. She strips naked not stopping at her underwear.

"Why are you wearing a necklace?" she asks.

"I don't want to lose it."

They hold each other on the couch, and Cathy conspires against his defenses with kindness, strokes his head, kisses his closed eyes, entangles him in softness.

"I thought you were going to turn out to be some kind of villain," he says.

"Because I'm promiscuous?"

He sleeps like Lazarus into late morning, wakes up alone on the couch, touches a scab above his eye. A tumult of memories spin to a single point, a clarity of now: he is neither late for watch nor abandoned in an American port, the ship within sight but out of reach, a fleck of metal on the ocean, no larger than the nearest seagull.

He is on vacation. He brokered it in the chief's office before visiting the travel agency.

"Can't lose you," the chief had told him, while puffing strenuously on a yellowed bone pipe that was once white. "Not even for a week."

"I'm overdue."

"That's a problem. Not mine."

"I'm sick. We're shut down. I'm only asking for a week."

The chief had held firm until Lucien brought efficiency into the argument. It wasn't efficient having someone so sick on the job. One week and he'd be better. They owed him the time.

"One week," he'd agreed. "And you'd better come back healthy." The chief was committed to efficiency. He'd divorced over it twice.

He hasn't coughed yet, and that's a small victory, doesn't feel poisoned by exhaustion. Still, the logistics of making coffee seem outrageously complicated. Into his second pot, he considers people he might contact and crosses out names as soon as he's written them down: Sylvia? No, from what Cathy said, she still holds a grudge. Cathy? No, if she knew, she would have said. Maybe Dave? Maybe.

The apartment still mystifies him. It's not just the photograph in the living room. In every room, something is off. The feeling of the tilting of an axis under the thumb of time. Representation become both fixed and strange. Things reduced to things. The sort of world in which an urn holding ashes is pottery. Like coming back home to find the windows curtained in newsprint of the corner store where he shopped for years for trivialities. The date above the headlines: the day he went to sea. In the weeks before he left, no one spoke to him about the store's failure. Like coming home to discover he was no longer a regular in his regular bar, the staff having changed while he was at sea.

Wandering through an apartment that does not know him, he imagines a body behind the curtain, feet sticking out, identity unknown. His.

He brings his third pot of coffee into the bathroom, sets it on the closed toilet cover, and runs the bath hot. He scrubs himself and drains and refills and scrubs and drains and refills until the bath ring tells him he's down to clean dirt.

Someone knocks at the door—at first gently and then with increasing violence. He searches the room. No towels.

Cathy's back. "Interesting use for a coffee pot," she says. "I hope for the sake of your genitals it's empty." She shows him a grocery bag before unloading it onto the kitchen table: oranges, apples, bananas, a pineapple. "Are you any good at opening these? I'm lousy with the packaging."

"When did you go?"

"I don't know. My watch beeped at seven and I'm a wiz at getting out of men's apartments quickly. My walk of shame is brisk."

"What time is it now?"

"One."

"I must be getting better. Still haven't coughed."

"Eat your fruit." She pulls a bottle from her purse. "Vitamin C. Take one. They're chewable so they're fun."

"Where have you been?"

"School. Tuesday's I've scheduled for my science pre-req. Geology. Just think: the end of the world is always at hand. All it takes is one good volcano."

"Do you have a friend named Dave?"

"You've met him."

"Do you think he'd have Olivia's Toronto address?"

"He doesn't."

"How do you know?"

"Why would she give her address to him? If you want Olivia's address and you think she's in Toronto, your best bet is to go to the library and lay hands on a Toronto phonebook."

"Of course she's in Toronto. She says she's in Toronto. Where else could she be?"

"Anywhere... here..."

"Cathy?"

"Un huh."

"Can I trust you?"

"Nope."

"But you're helping me?"

"Get better."

"Why?"

"Because you'll get over her. When you do I want you healthy. Tell you what, you stay here and get better. On my way to my night class I'll check out the library. There's phonebooks in the Killam that might be more recent. I'll try that and the main branch on Spring Garden. If I think of anything else, I'll let you know."

"You understand that grief doesn't keep a schedule. I can grieve for as long as I want to."

"It's not grief if you were together less than a month. It's ego. Vanity. Don't make those faces! Do you want to do it?"

"No!"

"Okay. I have to go anyway."

"Good-bye."

"Don't be mean. We don't get to own people. We just visit. The problem with you is that you don't understand that we're all tourists. Everything outlasts us. We're just taking pictures and tasting new foods and buying knickknacks. We stay longer in some places than in others, but the end is always the same."

"What's that?"

"Death. Every relationship ends in death. All we have is time, not people. Do you know Shah Jahan? He built the Taj Mahal and it's still here. He's not."

She calls at supper. The most recent phonebook is at Dal. Olivia's name is not in it.

He trudges to a bar within range of the harbour, where he spends a long time nursing three shots of rum. Near midnight he heads for the spot where he and Olivia first sat silently coming to an understanding. Turning a downtown corner, he sees a brown skinned woman dressed too smutty for Vegas negotiating into the open window of a Colt, watches her get into the car.

Lucien plays the conversations endlessly.

"I don't think love is forgetting," he says in one of his memories. "I don't think it's a turning off. At least that's not my idea of love. You know, the teenage thing that grownups do of letting desire champion reason."

"You believe in a reasoned desire."

"Why not? I don't actually need anyone in my life. If I put someone in my life I should desire them within reason. People are trouble. They should be good trouble."

"If?" she says. "Don't joke."

He wonders now how he could have been so stupid, so frivolous with their time together.

"I'm sorry." He might have said that.

"My cousin was essentially me, the same great expectations, and she's sunk."

"What happened to her won't happen to you."

"Even though we've only spoken twice in ten years I trust her probably more than anyone other than you. She's seen it all. You can't go through what she's gone through and not care. Not caring would kill you..."

"I promise that won't happen."

He should have let her talk. He punches his pillow, mutters, "Stupid, stupid, stupid."

The morning clouds are porous, leaking sun. Beams push warmly against Lucien's face. He discovers himself on the couch. In his restlessness he had abandoned the bed—not a place where he could sleep. He picks a letter off the floor. He's been afraid of it, afraid Harry's exuberance will tilt things.

The letter is unadulterated Harry: partial in its knowledge, optimistically firm in its belief that everything happens for a reason, but not for the providential reasons of Holy James. Harry's divine principle knows no God-willed punishment.

The letter is a wrecking ball of affability, a might-have-been of news from the world that isn't, the world inside the volcano. Lucien realizes there is another letter, one he hasn't seen but which must have been sent. Olivia somehow received it and replied and Harry is responding. Whatever Olivia wrote to Harry, her letter gave no hint of the coming debacle. She must have told Harry about her new classes, but not about the pregnancy. Harry's reply is to advise her to get Lucien to teach her the philosophy of *all the world's a bottle opener* for her coming exam.

The postscript reads, "I applied to do winter lay-up on the *Douglas*. It's only a week's work or maybe two, but I've spoken to the company and I'll go only if the *Douglas* lays-up in Halifax."

The sun is blocked again, the room in shadow. He switches on the light.

He returns the letter to its envelope and sets it on the bookshelf, takes a Cathy orange from the dining room table. The apartment still seems wrong. He wonders what Olivia did with the extra key.

Never in his childhood imaginings did Lucien picture himself soliciting a prostitute in a blizzard. The three women hunched in an alcove of the Post Office have already instructed him to bugger off. A fourth ranges freely. She wears a parka and an expression of persecution. The drawstrings on her hood are tightened so that she eyes him through a polyester periscope.

"Why are you looking for her?"

"I just want to talk."

"No." She shakes her head. "You're lying."

"I want to buy her. How much does she cost?"

"You want me to pimp for Maud? If it's an all-nighter you want, be a darling, my tits are freezing."

"Will you tell her that Lucien is looking for her?" He's written his number on a scrap of paper, which he produces from his pocket.

"Ten bucks."

Then he sets up at a bar with a good window looking out on Hollis. The place is a trap for Nova Scotia College of Art and Design students. It's the most promiscuous bar he knows when the weather allows. The bartender wears a Hawaiian shirt. He's a thin man with a Tom Selleck moustache.

"Come for the poetry?" he asks. "Open mic tonight."

"I'd rather something on tap."

"Don't like poetry?"

"I'll let you know."

A woman and a man are setting up the microphone under a picture of Marilyn Monroe overdramatizing, pushing her dress down with a Humboldt expression of milkmaid licentiousness. The man at the mic is exceptionally hairy. He wears a green *Monkees'* toque, taps the mic and makes it *thuck*.

"Can you hear me?" *Thuck*. "Can you hear me?" *Thuck*. *Thuck*.

Lucien points to himself and mouths, "Me?"

"Yeah." Of course, yeah. There's no one else. A blizzard pounds on the window. "Can you hear me?"

He nods.

Thuck. Thuck. Thuck. "Okay." *Thuck.* "I just wrote this poem. It's called 'Everything is Binary.' If you know Lacan, you'll get it."

The storm has whipped the street empty. The women have gone; no one is fishing with smiles, casting for johns. The bartender eyes Lucien with an expression of grievance. The man at the mic raps a poem about suicide followed by a poem about his distrust of the aged. Then one on religion, death, and small-minded women. The capper, "Awash in Blue, Blue, Blue," is a screed on Reagan, Thatcher, and Mulroney. The man's reading voice is deep and velvet, lulling.

"What did you think?" the bartender asks Lucien as the Monkee-man receives a kiss from the woman replacing him at the mic.

"Not much."

"Well, I have to let them keep reading."

"Why?"

"You're here. If there's a customer I can't kick them out."

Lucien downs his drink. Behind the bar is a postmodern picture of a man with a broken head. Lucien gestures towards it. "Is that good?"

Thuck. Thuck. Thuck. It's the woman's turn.

The bartender replies. "Don't like art?"

"What is art?"

"No one can answer that."

"Why are there art schools?"

"Art schools are about how, not why. Art just is."

"Is that picture beautiful?"

"It's not meant to be beautiful. Not everything that's beautiful is beautiful. The Hindenburg Disaster for instance."

"You paint that?" says Lucien.

"You think I'd be working here if I didn't?"

The woman at the mic says, "This poem is called 'Beware the Water.'"

And when I am parched for your love
humbled and emptied
you bring the water
push me in gladly
hold my face down till my eyes bulge.

A downed street sign on Lower Water signals the city's become dangerous and basic. The white-out forces itself into the sleeves of his jean jacket, onto his neck, bites at his scalp, forcing him to brush it off his hair every half block. It ices his breath, stoops his reflection in darkened windows as it rattles Marley-chains or No Parking signs. Snakes of snow scurry across the road. Blowing drifts stopple narrow sidewalks making his steps deliberate and slow. A university-age waiter peers out the window of a seafood restaurant. He wears a black shirt and pants under the green-apron uniform of the establishment. His hair is pulled in a tight ponytail, his eyes dulled from looking.

Lucien arrives at the dock in a blinding absence of swirling pitch black specks of white made visible by streetlamps. The whiteness of white assaults his eyes with their ice cold sameness. He cups his hand, squints.

He remembers her feet making slow circles above the water.

"Is this what it's like to be a sailor?"

"It's more like that."

The lights of Eastern passage will not penetrate the storm. Only the empty anger, the vacuity of the wind abounds with a gale-force intensity. He's trying to hurt himself. It's working. The nearest waves are capped white. They flounder and flail like drowning philosophers. To starboard, a baby tree grows out of a half-submerged rock, a two-foot sapling that, in its quest to put down roots, has split a rock neatly in two. Slender, dead-leafy, an abundance of nothing become an abundance in nothing, insinuating itself into a crevice, making a rock consort with life.

"Me?"

He has to pee.

Sliding up is impossible. He grips rough edges—parking meters, street signs, and parked cars—negotiating his way up an icy incline towards Barrington. Under the cupolas of Wormwood's Dog and Monkey Theatre he stamps and warms. Spring Garden Road is empty. At the Tower Road Apartments he sees a light glowing yellow in Olivia's old apartment. A new tenant has replaced her. Robie Street kills him. He can't stop the freeze, walks backwards in the middle of the street, hands jammed in his pockets when his fingers ice and he can't cup them to his forehead.

He can feel his resistance giving way. The pain of walking gives way to clarity.

On either side nest abandoned churches, frozen-shut mailboxes, drug stores, boarding houses. Wooden building block homes run the gamut of primary colours, all two-stories high in obedient parallels.

Like Olivia, he didn't care much for the architecture when he first arrived but that wasn't what worried him most. He'd been hired on a freighter, stuck with it till a better ship was available, signed ship's articles at the same rank, and then was on to the next. In that manner, he turned sideways, always, in his career, never advancing. The first year in Halifax, he knew no one. At the end of each day he found himself defeated, ostracized, and exhausted. You could not live in Halifax a stranger and not pay for something unless you kept moving. He began reading in bars. It was Sylvia who made the city real. She brought him into rooms and conversations he'd been shut out of. But the conversations were bits of nothing, Sylvia-kindnesses, suffocating in a kindly way.

By Black Street his legs are ice. He counts down the houses: four, three, two, one, home. The lock is trouble, but he gets it at last, falls to the floor, his head warming to the room, slowly exchanging the metaphysical for the material: ranked books, dying plant, picture on the wall, hypodermic needle under the couch.

6. December

He's a reverse Timothy Leary. He tuned out, turned off, and dropped in.
—Said by a legal-aid lawyer at the annual Lieutenant Governor's Garden Party on the Government House lawn.

HE WAKES UP on the floor, the phone ringing. It's his mother. "Is something wrong?"

"Everything's good."

"Your voice is funny."

"Probably the connection."

"No. It's the eighties. Connections are good."

Someone is knocking.

"Mother, I have to put down the phone to get the door."

"It's business hours. Twelve cents a..."

"I won't *be* a minute."

"You know how much we hate throwing..."

"I do."

"...bottomless pit..."

He drops the receiver on the couch and opens the door to a bundled woman in a pea coat, a scarf wrapped about her face. She has Olivia's eyes.

He waves her in, pats his lips with a finger, picks up the phone.

"...disgraceful..."

"Something's up. Can I call later or tomorrow?"

"No need. If you're alive, that's good enough."

"I'm alive. I love you, Mother."

"Prove it. Write a letter. With content."

The woman unwraps down to the same lips as Olivia. Her expression lacks expression. "I've been waiting for you to get home," she says flatly.

"You got my message?"

"What message?"

In over a decade at sea he's been in an enclosed space with only one other prostitute—in the cab when he was eighteen.

"Do you want coffee?"

"No, I've a ways to go. I've come to tell you my price: five hundred, eighty-seven dollars for the whole night."

"Five hundred and eighty-seven dollars?"

"I'll be here after ten. Got it?"

"Is that your normal price?"

"No. Have you started something with that blondie-skank who keeps coming by? Send her away tonight. I don't react well to her *type*."

"I don't know how to get out of seeing her."

She rewraps in her scarf. "Take it from me, with most things, the way in is the way out."

The VW gypsy caravan held a thin, foam mattress, a half-full open beer cooler, several stars and moons cut from cardboard and covered in tin foil. They hung from strings attached to the ceiling and had been sized to give an illusion of perspective, the ones up front larger than the ones behind. The thin, hooked-nosed man in the Satan's Choice jacket had gathered the cards, the reading over. An expression of confusion splashed across his face.

"Which way she is up?"

"Do you mean facing?"

"I mean she—the last card."

He flipped through the deck, found the woman in the diaphanous dress and placed her on the counter. "This way?" This way was right-side up. "Or this?" Upside down.

"This way. The right way," said Harry.

"No," said Lucien, "the other."

"Either of you for sure?"

Harry and Lucien looked at each other. Both said, "Yes."

"*Maudit*," exhaled the man. He reached into the cooler behind him, pulled out a can of *50* and opened it. "You two beat the cake." He took a long drink.

"What does it matter which way the card faces?" said Harry. "It's still the same picture."

"Two readings. I show..." He had to kick a pile of Alisteir Crowley books across the floor of the van to get at the paperback beneath, *The Pictorial Key to the Tarot* by A. E. Waite. The cover revealed, under the symbol for infinity, a robed man in a blaze of yellow triumphantly holding a white phallus. The hook-nosed man thumbed to a dog-eared page, mumbling as he read, then set the book on his knee, craning to bookmark it with his elbow. "This way—" He placed the card right side up. "She is nature, mutter—motherhood, fretility." He was reading upside down, biting hard on his accent. "This way—" He turned the card around, contorting himself to keep his page. "She is..." He gestured to the sentence with his nose: dependence, smothering, lack of self-reliance.

"Why didn't you say that before?" said Harry.

"*Crisse de câlice de tabarnak d'esti de sacrament!*"

"Such language," said Lucien. "His English was perfect a minute ago."

"Creepy," said Harry.

"*C'est l'erreur*, okay? The cards 'ave best meaning. When you read your own. This my first time try to read someone else. 'Ave to 'ave magic power." He pantomimed pulling a rabbit from his beer. "I don't do except for money."

"Maybe it won't matter which way the card was."

"Won't matter? *Esti d'épais à marde!* I tell you la différence."

He seemed bottled up, frustrated, lost for a language. He looked around for one in the park then on the sidewalk, where the walking women were at their task, repeatedly passing La Terrace Picardie.

"You watch *les films?*"

They nodded.

"Do you know *l'amour*...*les* love *film?*"

"Yes," they said.

"Blanchette Brunoy? No? María Casares? No? Ginette Leclerc? Simone Signoret? No? You say you 'as watched movies. *L'étoile du Nord* is. Playing down the street. If about *l'amour*, every movie about which way the card she dealt."

"How do you mean?" said Harry.

"In every story. A man ee wants *l'amour*. You know this?" He hugged himself and kissed his arms, the red flames of his decal riding up his shoulders. "Ees dealt Empriss card upside down. And plot of *le film*. Ee 'as to turn card so right."

"I still don't get you," said Harry. "Do you know any English movies?"

"*Casablanca?*"

"Yeah."

"*Roman Holiday? North by Northwest? Arthur?*"

They nodded.

"*Bon*. Each of those movies. Start with Empriss this way. Humphry Bogart. Ee turn card *comme ça*. Then ee in charge. *C'est tout*. Now can shoot bad guy. Boom. Boom. Happy ending. Maybe ee go back to first woman."

"The French woman he dumps in the bar? Marlene?" said Lucien.

"'As better legs, I tink."

"I guess. Yeah."

"I don't think that paradigm holds true," said Harry.

"Paradigm? What it is?"

"Pattern."

"When it isn't pattern?"

"James Dean does nothing to Natalie Wood in *Rebel Without a Cause*. That's a love story. I think."

"I know *le film*." He crosses his arms, considers Harry's rebuttal. "Means is about parents."

"You're making that up."

"*Le film* end with father saying *câlice* to mother. Why there? *Parce que une* woman with *contrôle…ou…commande* 'as to be… *impuissante*. Do you know that?"

"No," said Harry, "but I get your meaning. Every movie is *The Taming of the Shrew*. An independent woman has to be made dependent. So you're saying that because it's the mother in *Rebel Without a Cause* who needs to be taken down a peg, ergo, the movie must be about the parents. I can't remember if that's inductive or deductive reasoning. The one that doesn't work. Sorry. Don't buy it."

He shrugged. "We live *comme ça—comme le film*. Same in *Casablanca*, Same in *It Happened One Night*. Do you know that one?"

They shrugged.

"All about love coming at night."

She arrives after midnight smelling like *PineSol*. Above the knees, she is dressed shop-girl plain in a crew neck sweater and Gloria Vanderbilt jeans, a green scarf threaded through her belt loops. Her black boots, long and leather, are comfortingly bourgeoisie. Angled on the floor, she removes them with vaudevillian impropriety, stretching her legs above her head one at a time, pulling them off in a single, assertive motion. She is desirably slender and busty, her expression hard as a legal judgement, her pout pushes a parenthetical wrinkle around her lips. All day, he has laboured to entrench himself in arguments. It astonishes him how easily she destroys the security of reasoning by awakening desire in him. He feels her challenge in his throat. An animal want. Her open stare mocks him.

"You have the money?"

He does. Six sweat-dampened one hundred dollar bills he's been worrying for half an hour. She folds the bills evenly, tries to wedge them into a tight jean pocket. Then she retrieves her purse from the front hall and drops it on the couch, stuffs the money in, and begins taking out Saltines and Lifesavers, a flashlight, a paperback with no cover, an orange, a black hood, and, finally, a change purse.

She counts the thirteen dollars into his hand. "I assumed you'd have exact change." She repacks her purse. "The bathroom. This could take a while. Order Chinese while I'm gone. I don't care what you get. Just no chicken balls. It's not food. Something, anything with almonds."

As she passes the table she stops to touch the deck of tarot cards he bought that afternoon at a magic shop on Prince. The pack lies open, cards spilled carelessly.

"Oh yeah," she says, "no fortune cookies. I find them offensive."

Then she's in the bathroom and he's phoning for food, anxiously over-ordering to safeguard against omissions. Occasionally she opens a tap. He pulls down a *Reeds: On Steam Engineering Knowledge for Marine Engineers* and stumbles up and down a paragraph until his anxiety abates.

When the valve starts to close down, the ventilation to atmosphere of the steam from chamber A will be stopped. This causes a pressure build up in the chamber which assists closing of the valve. The additional closing force due to this arrangement would be approximately equal to the pressure in chamber A multiplied by $(D2 - d2)n/4$.

Mind over nature. Soothing. She turns on the tap, and he flips absently to a cautionary page: don't add water to an empty boiler with the fires up. Bank the burners and wait. A failing question on the fourth's exam. A picture shows a smashed firetube that would have been a surprise to the five men standing watch—a watertender, fireman, oiler, dayman, engineer. The ones in the boiler room killed in the blast, in the rush of steam, the others scalded to death.

She emerges wet and washed. Looking, *sans*-makeup, not-necessarily-older.

"What do you want to know?"

"I want to know why Olivia is doing this to me."

"Doing? She's doing nothing to you. As I understand it, you two are done."

She is up again. At the table. Touching cards.

"I didn't figure you for a mystic. Would I meet a stranger if you did my cards?"

"I can't read them. I was just testing them."

"For what?"

"I'll show you." He goes to the table and spreads the cards at random. He gathers them, shuffles, and lays out twelve-cards.

"Look at them carefully."

Again he scatters then gathers the cards. Shuffles. Lays them out in a twelve-card spread.

"Not the same," he says.

"No," she agrees.

"I've been dealing hands all afternoon. They're never the same."

"So?"

"How can you have more than one future? If the tarot knows what will happen, the cards have to always be the same."

"Spoken like an engineer. That's not how it works. The cards can be talking about different things."

"When I had my cards read in Sorel, the man predicted you."

"Predicted me? How clever."

"He said I'd dealt myself a wicked hand."

She says, "Yes."

"You've been in this apartment before."

"What makes you say that?"

Lucien goes to the bookshelf. Returns with the needle.

"Yours I think."

She fingers it gingerly and nods. "Could be mine. There's a lot of junkies on this planet. If we organized as a voting bloc things would change."

"What were you doing here?"

"Olivia sent me."

"Why?"

"She lost something."

"She could have come herself."

"I wouldn't let her."

"But you let yourself come. And you didn't just look. You alphabetized my books."

"Did I? I don't remember."

"You arranged them by titles not authors."

"That's crazy. You'll want to get that."

"What?"

"The food, I imagine."

He watches her eat, artfully, like someone who is used to being watched. He has always had trouble dining with strangers. He can slice and chew, but, if he imagines people watching, he can't swallow. He once caught a ship and didn't eat for three days while trying to get to know the crew well enough to stand their gaze.

She says, "The money you owed me was for a trip to Montréal. The fare and the motel."

"Who is in Montréal?"

"A doctor friend."

"Was Olivia sick?"

"In a way."

"What way?"

"In the way I was once sick, a long time ago."

"What kind of sick?"

"The kind of sick that doesn't make you stronger and that doesn't go away for eighteen years."

"I don't understand."

"I think you do. I couldn't trust you to do right by Olivia." She picks up her fork. "So I took her to the same doctor I had..." She puts down her fork. "But she'd changed her mind. I wouldn't let her. I'd made her promise that the decision would be mine and I held her to that promise. Afterwards, when she turned on me, I wanted to know I wasn't wrong. That's why I came back here. I was looking for assurances that you were a creep." She laughs. "Instead you turned out to be me."

"We have nothing in common."

"Oh, yeah. We're not real people, you and me. We just inhabit people. But we're not them. We pattern ourselves off them because we don't know who we are. I know that because I inhabited you."

"I'm not you. Do you think I'd abort someone else's child! Jesus, what right did you have to talk her into it?"

"I love her, that's what gives me the right. You were seeing another woman."

"What? I wasn't seeing anyone else."

"That's not what blondie said."

"Blondie?"

"That skank who spends her nights with you."

"What did she say?"

"She told Olivia she was still seeing you, that you were talking marriage. It broke Olivia."

"It isn't true!"

"*You* told Olivia you were seeing her."

"I had seen her. Once. It was over before Olivia and I started."

"Then why would blondie say it? Why would she say that word? Why would she mention marriage?"

"To elbow Olivia out of the way."

"People don't do that. Not with so much on the line. Why would she hate Olivia so much she would…"

"It wasn't hate! She didn't know Olivia was pregnant."

"No one hurts another person that much except out of hatred."

"You've got her wrong. That's not her sort of passion."

"If not hatred, then what?"

"Tourism."

They've been sitting together holding hands in silence. She lets go of his hand and holds hers out to reveal a tremor.

"At a certain age," she says, "the ones who've made bad choices and the ones who've been unlucky resemble each other."

"When does that happen?"

"About midnight." She props her arm against the back of the couch and leans into it. She fidgets. She stands up, takes off her shirt, pulls a needle from her purse, injects herself under her breast.

He has seen many things. Nothing this raw.

She inspects her breast. Smells under her arms.

"It's terrible having a body. I remember how embarrassed I was the first time I bought deodorant. You don't live with the threat. Your body is your own. But Olivia and me… The most common cause of death for women is men. I inject in my breast because no one looks there. People know you by your worst transgressions. If my johns knew I was an addict, they wouldn't know what to do with the information. They're rough enough. To them my body is the body of a prostitute. What restraint would they show the body of an addict? No, thank you. I don't want to die that particular way."

She roams the apartment turning off lights.

"You're not a real sailor, are you?"

"What do you mean?"

"I've known sailors. You're different."

The street casts a pale glow through the curtainless kitchen window. Even when she stumbles she is dreadfully gorgeous. In the slight window glow she casts a shadow that haunts the room, sliding into contours, ineloquent and knowing.

She says, "Olivia is beautiful, don't you think?"

He is struck by how desirable her shape is in shadow.

"I'm not sure I know what beauty is."

"Oh, that's easy."

She is in the bathroom where the curtainless window above the tub most fully admits the full moon. She stands outside his vision but he can see the dark of her on the hallway floor, arms busy with her torso. He can imagine her form as she peers at the mirror lifting her breast, determining whether the new mark shows.

"Beauty is uncertainty." She tosses back her shadow hair. "What does anyone feel when they encounter perfection?"

"Joy?"

"No, not joy."

"What then?"

"Inadequacy." Her shadow takes off its shirt. Slides out of its jeans. "That's how you know you've encountered beauty. When it makes you feel small, horrible, empty."

She is back in the hall, addressing him directly.

"I, for instance, am beautiful."

He looks away.

"Olivia adores you. I didn't realize. It wouldn't have changed things. What happened had to be done. The abortion was a lot harder than we expected. She lost blood—couldn't stop bleeding. That never happened to me. She spent two days in a cheap ward and it got to her. We'd just gotten back when you called. I had to coach her. She couldn't say the right things."

"Which were?"

"I have to finish my degree. I can't make the wrong choice. You would have stopped me and called it love. All I have is what I'm able to make and you will love me into a cage. I would never be free to say no to anyone.

"She sent me for a necklace. She was sick. Depressed. Angry. I didn't know she was going to hate me. I did the right thing. She wanted something to touch. I never found it. She wanted to look for herself. I told her I'd lost the key, but I lived here. I walked in you. Saw you. I like your mother. Her letters are funny."

She leads him to the bedroom and turns on the light, and shows him the needle holes below her breast.

"I'm probably the first woman you've met with a tattoo. Don't be surprised if, in the future, everyone has a tattoo. She wanted something to touch. She sent me but I couldn't find it. She wouldn't stop crying, so I touched her. I shouldn't have done that. She shouldn't have let me. She did so she could hate me. I like your mother. I like the way she told you about converting your bedroom to a sewing room. Ten years and she finally got around to it and feels guilty. You've got to tell her that it's okay. And you've got to tell her you're not coming back. Ever. She doesn't get that. She thinks this sailing thing is a phase and you'll come back and take over the farm."

She laughs: "Imagine showing up at the door with Olivia! A brown woman and a mixed child in a white farming community? Fun. Come. I owe you something." She throws off the last of her clothing, a pair of red lace panties, stands rocking, naked. He is drawn to her nakedness, the curve of her ass, her flat stomach and full tits. She lies back on the bed, follows his eyes and spreads her legs slightly, watches him look, "I don't know what's right," she says. "Let us lay together or lie together, as the case may be."

He watches her get up in the morning. No good-byes, just the same question he's been asking all night.

"Why?"

She says, "The why I could answer I did. The one you're asking now you should save for church. I'm the furthest thing from a priest. Or not. I hear a lot of confessions but I don't give absolutions."

He listens to her in the hall by the door, rewrapping, pulling on her boots, a statement in sounds articulated out of sight, hears her say, "You passed the test. I think it was honourable of you not to fuck me last night. Anyone else would have done it. No one ever wants to cuddle." Then she is gone.

The phone rings. Lucien staggers to it to hear the chief say, "You're in. Hallelujah! I'm going to have to rescind my offer. The steamship inspector is in Friday at eight. He wants to see the blades on the turbine. We haven't gotten the cover up yet. I need you for four just to be sure that everything's together."

"You can't do this to me. Not now…"

"No choice."

"You're stealing the only thing I own. All I have is time."

"What you have is time and a job. You'll only have time if you're not in at four on Friday."

"I'm not coming in."

"You will, Luci. You always do."

<hr />

II

A cadet on the *Soo River Trader,* he spent mornings on watch looking out the gangway door, seeing the river wake up—the St. Lawrence below Montréal. Reeds and fog. Lights blinking on one at a time. One dark morning, a dog barked, challenging the *Trader*'s passage. He couldn't see the dog. It remained a sound. He tried to memorize the bark, assuming every day had to matter.

Later that summer he heard a second dog. He'd gone to sleep as the ship steamed up the Saguenay in the direction of Tracy; woke up in the larger of two towns sharing a bridge. Not Tracy—just somewhere. It was noon and he had four hours. He was wandering the downtown—three steeples, one stoplight (not-Tracy was one of those towns where Catholicism or aluminum is the main industry)—trying to find a place to sit where he wouldn't have to talk to anyone.

Thinking on a park bench, trying not to be seen, he became aware of trouble, followed the smell of smoke to the river, saw it thicken and curtain the far shore. Another three steeples stood above the smoke looking back at the three on his side. He heard later that, after the fire, there were only two.

A dog barked balefully across the river, unseen, the "I am here" of an animal. For years he thought he'd wake up one day in a place he couldn't name, a place with two steeples, and would know the town by its bark. For a decade, he willed the sound to return, aggressive, challenging, above all, familiar.

He is intimate with the thrust of a two-stroke Sulzer RND 76, the clackity clackity clackity of a four-stroke Burmeister & Wain. He's never worked on a Cat, but its unhinged whine is familiar from all the other times he's taken the Dartmouth ferry. It's his recovery trip. He takes it as a stopgap on depression. Fifteen minutes of engine sounds.

Captain Kyle is visible in the wheelhouse but hasn't seen him. He's preoccupied with the same trip he's made a thousand times: a straight line from Halifax to Dartmouth; a straight line back. Lucien can imagine dots in the water, in Captain Kyle's mind, to be connected by their wake. A white pencil-stroke on a green page. He watches McNabs adjust its shape to the passing perspective of the ferry. Knows that what he's looking for isn't off the port or starboard bow. It can't be seen from this ship, but the familiar vibration and stutter of the hull on molehill waves can nevertheless bring it into view.

Someone is tapping metal on glass. He peers about the deck at the muffled passengers, and the sound becomes insistent. Captain Kyle has seen him. They make eye contact. Captain Kyle nods. Lucien nods back.

Lucien wonders what it means to hold a captain's rank piloting people back and forth between two ports within sight of each other. What does it mean to wage so repetitive a life in a career that conjures notions of adventure? Since arriving on the coast Lucien has seen scores of Captain Kyles, the younger ones in sailors' bars and union halls, the older ones in legions. Men in love with the mystique of sailing, who know their performances are false. Men who crave order over freedom—who talk about the mystery of the sea but would rather be in port with a beer and a book. When he first decided on sailing, Lucien hoped that one day a ship would take him to Iceland. It was how he excused the job to himself. His ships held the possibility of a marvelous voyage like a tiny shard of childhood, a stowaway in the cargo.

The sound of a dark barking.

His voice.

Cut off, disembodied, a thing…

It was on his third ship, the *Norman M. Paterson*, that he heard the tree story, a test of credulity told up and down the Seaway to new engine room hands. He heard it from his supervisor, the fourth engineer, who spent the summer telling Lucien he was brainless. "You're an instant *ingineer*," the fourth assured him regularly. "Just add water." To the fourth, who was fifty and had never risen above the rank of fourth due to a career crippling disability—he could not divide fractions and could not be taught—to be an engineer meant starting with a mop not with a book. The job was for men and real men did not do math.

Early that browbeaten summer he told Lucien a story about an engineer on a lake steamship that broke down on the Saguenay. "Brokin pistin rod. Wach you gotta figure is there's nothin' 'round but trees. The engineer grabs a few of the crew, takes a lifeboat ashore, and chops up the straightest tree for miles. He turns it on the lathe and puts in the ingine. A woodin pistin rod. A few hours later, hey Bub, the ship is on its way. That's an *ingineer*. You won't find that in a book."

In a book, no, but Lucien later discovered that all down the Seaway, from Thunder Bay to Baie Comeau, people told the same story again and again and again. Sometimes it was dressed up. The trunk was still alive. That was Lucien's favourite version of a colourful lie. In this version, the engine room did a refit some months later and discovered the piston had grown a branch with buds and leaves. He liked to think of the engine room living.

In his rounds, he sometimes heard a bark, a trick of frequency. Sounds colliding and combining. And then, one night, he had a dream. He dreamt the engine room was made of trees. Everything that moved and pounded and whirred. Different types of wood. And the stack had no smoke. No slick of oil followed their wake down the seaway.

"Everyday matters," he told Harry the first week of their friendship. The *Douglas* was stopped for repairs. They were climbing out of the engine room after a fourteen-hour shift. They had a two hour reprieve before standing a regular four-hour watch and Harry said, "How do you sleep for this job?"

"You're not going to sleep. You're going ashore. Every day counts. You can't write it off. We're going ashore. We're going to buy a beer and drink it walking back to the ship."

In a dépanneur they picked up two Laurentides and a French paper, which they couldn't read. From the pictures and the English-looking words Harry grasped that the guitarist for The Pretenders had died.

"Did you know him—James Honeyman Scott?"

"Good name for a rock star," Lucien said, "The king of Arabia died three days ago. Did you know that?"

"How could that be important?"

"How could the death of a rock star be important?"

"He overdosed on drugs."

He remembers on an afternoon in August still-hunting with Olivia in the gallery. A one-a-day 1928 painting of a blue soldier backgrounded in blue holds them, the soldier at ease, his expression a question.

Olivia says, "Imagine having the presence of art to make this."

She gets up from the bench they've shared in silence, stands breathably close to the canvas, lets it fill her vision. "I had something terrible happen to me one time. I will tell you this story one day. I was in physical pain and I was grieving and I went for a walk. It was grey and it was rainy. There was a rainbow and there were ripples and it was like the whole world was ripples. The clouds, the rainbow, the searing pain... I don't get where it comes from, the power to make art, to make beauty. But I often think that if you can grieve, you can *see* beauty. Both are intensely personal acts."

The painting is entitled *Bleu Sur Bleu*. The soldier on the wall wears a blue army coat over a blue uniform, blue breeches, blue French boot socks rising past his knees. His left hand rests in his pocket, clips his army coat open like a drapery tieback to reveal a wide belt black as his black shoes. His right hand hangs by his side.

They fucked twice that morning, and he can still feel her, the imprint of memory touching inside while he admires her posture, her baggy-corduroy beauty. He knows the immediacy of her, knows how it feels to hold her ass in one hand, lifting while thrusting into her, knows the sound of her breath, her voice in his ear, the sound of his name spoken in that way.

Olivia says:

"Do you know about comas? If you go into a coma for a week or even a few hours, your joints calcify. It can take months to rehabilitate and fully use your limbs again after even a brief coma. So it is with people. They go into spiritual comas and the pain of rehabilitation, if they have the imagination to attempt it, is too great. They stay emotionally calcified. When you said I might be beautiful in the bar after how mean I'd been I thought, 'Maybe I'm not calcified.' You never know. There was good reason to fear I might be. Someone always has to tell you. Sleepers dream they're awake."

The eyes beneath the blue French army cap hold an unspoken challenge.

"Friend or enemy?" Lucien says. "That's what he's thinking, but he's not going to ask. He'll make up his own mind."

He can smell their sex or he imagines it.

"What does he decide when he looks at you?" she asks.

"I don't know. *I* like *him*."

7. December

i used to live in the middle of
nowhere   your
departure brought me
back again
—Poem graffitied in a stall in the women's bathroom in the Department of Philosophy at Dalhousie University.

IT'S NOT 10 AM and the mall already smells like coffee and popcorn. He doesn't know how long he's been following when she surprises him, doubles back through the Sears perfume section and catches him sneaking. Her expression is not good.

"What is this?"

Sylvia wears a grey dress coat and a thin red scarf—more dash of colour than windbreak—black slacks, and leather shoe-boots. She dresses for her duties, not her whims. Unusual for Sylvia is the baby-sized purple mitten she holds. Everything else says she's coming home from the midnight-to-morning shift on the suicide hotline.

"Well?" she presses. When he doesn't answer she says, "You look like hell."

"I've been hearing that a lot."

"It's true. You look your age."

"No one looks thirty. Everyone looks twenty-five or forty."

"Boy, oh boy, you do like to trivialize. That's how it is with you. When in doubt, cut things with a clever-sounding absurdity to prove you can make meaning meaningless. It's a threat you know. You hold people in the cusp of your contempt and dare them to say something you don't agree with. You do it because you're afraid."

"Stop!" he cries. "Don't analyze me. I don't want it. I look like hell because I am hell. I was walking past, saw the mall opening, and came in to get warm. I've been walking all night. And here you are peering around corners. I know what you're doing. You're looking for the child who lost that mitten. I was looking, too. I was going to help."

"You were spying."

"I was keeping you in sight."

For a time she is quiet, then she touches his arm, says, "Come with me," and leads him out the store to a bench in front of a half-assembled Santa's farrago: a high-backed, red velvet throne, a sagging, grey slum-castle battlement.

"Sit down," she says. "Tell me."

"Are you my friend?"

She takes a deep breath. "Haven't you hurt me enough?"

"I didn't think you'd seen me. You were looking at things."

"It's a mall."

"You were looking at people."

"A mall with people. Go figure."

"Stop being mean! Just stop! I can't take it right now. Be upset with me any other time. If I'm the iceberg you've shipwrecked yourself on, okay. I wasn't trying to hurt you. Icebergs don't. I've been here since they opened the doors—an hour before the stores. I'm scared to be anywhere else. I hurt everywhere. I've been walking and the mall is warm. Jesus. Look at me. You want to..."

He stops when he realizes how wrong her eyes are, how waxy her cheeks. How long has she been holding her breath?

"I take that for a yes. You haven't hurt me enough." She says, "Jesus, Luci, one really has to weather the weird with you."

Several stores away, someone is opening up. A metal barrier clangs open.

"I am not weird."

"You are weird. I used to think you were just playing weird to keep your emotional distance. There could never be any true intimacy between us while you faked. But, no, you weren't faking. You'd be weird anywhere with anyone."

"Not with Olivia."

"Bullshit. Why did she break up with you?"

"Who said we broke up?"

"I can tell when my best friend is no longer seeing the man I wanted to give my life to. Call it *je ne sais what the fuck*."

Over the mall sound system, Judy Garland enjoins them to have a merry little Christmas. A woman grunts. A gate opens.

"I shouldn't have followed. I'm sorry. But stop with this. *Now*. You may be the only person in this town whose opinion of me matters. Revise it. Watching you look for a child to give that mitten was helping. I've been cold. You were doing something warm."

"Are you still talking?" Her expression vacillates between pain, anger, and jocularity as if she can't understand the genre of the play she's either in or watching. She throws up her hands. "Hold me."

"What?"

"Shut up and hold me. You'll get it."

Her shoulders are still. Her grip is tight. He can feel it, an invisible shudder she wants to reveal. He needs to investigate fully.

"Are you smelling me?"

"I wouldn't do that."

"Of course you would, Luci. You're the weirdest person I know. Okay. You weren't weird with Olivia. As I understand your stream-of-insensitivity that's supposed to make me feel better. So what happened? You had an affair and she dumped you. Is that right?"

"Why do you say that?"

"You're a sailor."

"I'm not a very good sailor."

"Then what?"

"Will you keep this secret?"

"Jesus." Sylvia gazes off in search of Him.

"Yes or no?"

"Yes. Damn it."

"She had an abortion."

"What is wrong with you?"

"What did I do?"

"That's not a parlour story. You don't tell that to people."

"You deal with this all the time."

"With strangers! Oh, right, you *are* a stranger. Olivia isn't."

"You are going to help me."

"Why would I do that?"

"Because I helped you. Remember?"

She stares into the child's mitten. "How?"

"I want her back. If she's the person I knew, she'll still want me. Her cousin talked her into aborting the baby while I was at sea."

"You want the impossible. People in a relationship where a fetus is aborted *do not* stay together. Luci, they can't. If a relationship is going to last it's going to be held together with memory. In a relationship where there's been an abortion memory is the enemy. And so long as they're together they remember." She shakes her head. "I don't get it. Why would her cousin... She must hate Olivia."

"She loves her."

"She says that she loves her?"

"Yes and I believe her."

"You're wrong. As far as I'm concerned, you're both certifiable, her cousin, too."

"That's your professional opinion? How many clients have you lost?" He holds a finger to his head and shoots her a look.

"Don't push me. Luci, you have to eat your suffering. There is nothing you can do. Let her go. That's philosophy. I'm telling you what you need to hear. It's true. Holding on to pain, to grief, won't bring back the dead. Everyone tries to do that. I know from personal experience. It doesn't work. If it did, only saints would walk the earth."

"I Can't Let Her Go."

Sylvia stands and straightens a wrinkle from her slacks. "That's what they all say." She drops the mitten into a trash can. "Then they do. I can't help you. It's too much. You want to talk to her when you don't even know the first thing about me? Had it been us, I would have kept the baby, you son of a bitch."

Soft snow on hardened boot prints edged in ice lead downtown. He treads in yesterday's traces, imagines doing the Atticus Finch, walking in another man's shoes. What does that mean, anyway, and why was *To Kill a Mockingbird* standard reading in farm-country Ontario high schools? The Canadian content wasn't much better. What he took from Margaret Atwood is that life is thoroughly symbolic. After studying *Surfacing* to its marrow in grade ten, for a scouting report on the future, he took to reading Carl Jung instead of the *Playboys* his friends passed round.

As he crosses Oxford, some of the recognizable patterns disappear, replaced by new. What looks like a small step for a man is someone burdened and slow he imagines, or a child with big feet. The women's prints could be Olivia's because why not? They lead to someone. Is this her step? Her walk is a quick stomp. Not a demonstration of anger but deliberation. Of course, the prints could just as well belong to Cathy; either possibility is equally improbable. Cathy walks like she talks, like she knows she's being watched, being listened to, if only by herself.

He turns the corner of Blower and, to his surprise, there she is/isn't. He thinks it's her, but it's only some sleight of association. A shapely woman in a white parka talks in broad gestures to a tall man with Jon's physique and posture. His expression isn't defeated enough to be Jon's but it doesn't matter. Lucien is taken off guard by a flash of jealousy. He walks past, confirms he doesn't know either, and thinks, *Why should I be possessive of Cathy?*

"That was a punch in the head."

Ten minutes later, he stands behind a tree outside Cathy's window, watching. He knows her schedule and she keeps it, leaves at the crack of noon with a strikingly neutral expression on her face. In her harp seal outfit, she looks bored, the swing of her hips, mechanical. She disappears into a group of pedestrians, strangers going her way.

When he gets home, Sylvia is on the step, still dressed for talking people out of self-harm. Her cheek says she's been crying. "We'll try this again," she tells him.

He makes tea. They sit at the dining room table.

"What's with the tarot?" says Sylvia. "Were you entertaining gypsies?"

"A prostitute."

"Of course you were. That's what sailors do."

"She was Olivia's cousin. Did you know she hooks? I bought her for the whole night."

"You can't tell me that's not weird."

"We didn't do it. We talked. She is the only person besides Olivia who knows what happened while I was at sea. All Olivia would tell me was that she'd lost the baby."

"That's not as dismal as you think. Olivia didn't want you to dislike her. That may be a good sign." She picks up the Death card, looks at it, tosses it back on the table. "Yes, it's a good sign."

"Sylvia, why are you here?"

"I was wrong. If you love Olivia, if you truly know her, it's not hopeless."

"Why the change of mind?"

"It's possible to love people through anything, if you're big enough."

"And you think she and I are?"

"Interesting question. Listen, if you want her back, start by being honest with yourself."

"How do I do that? I've spent the night wandering in the freezing cold trying to define that word. What is honesty?"

"Stop listening to your ego. Your ego is your enemy. Perception isn't truth. It's twisted, distorted by our defenses. By our egos. *Why* do you want her back? That's where you start. You didn't like her when you first met her. Remember how you embarrassed me? What did you see in her that changed your mind? That's what you want to reach. If you're honest."

"Her imagination isn't gutless."

"I like that." Sylvia touches more cards. Her fingers find the upside down Empress. She frowns and turns it. "Only talk to her once. As much as I love you, I won't have you stalking a friend. Do you agree? One conversation only."

"One conversation. But you don't have to tell me where she is. She never left."

"She didn't. That's a second good sign. You don't scare her." Sylvia stands. She wears an expression of relief. Smiling at the ceiling she says, "I did it."

"Did what?"

"Let go of you."

The season is cold and warm by turns.

The sidewalk on Robie is snowbanked to a single lane held by a ponderous woman. Her lethargy raises Lucien's anxiety. Slow to move, he is forced to think. *Think about something else*, he tells himself, but it's impossible. He storms past at the intersection on Quinpool. The day drips from eaves heavy with snow. Deep puddles block the sidewalks. By Tower Road, his feet have been soaked for several blocks. A summer bird chirps from a wire above.

The intercom is difficult. He presses twice, listens to fuzz, and wonders. Did she see him on the street? Is silence a knowledgeable response? A crack of static could mean she's pressed the intercom button. If she's waiting for him to leave or talk, she's waiting in a sunlit room with a window radiating comfort, waiting near the high, soft bed on which they were.

He says, "I'm here." Of course, she knows that if she's listening, damn it. "I'm going to say something and I'm going to leave. You don't have to speak. When I go I won't come back."

A movement outside the glass door: the lethargic woman stands on the other side. She looks much younger than he expected, high-school-drop-out age.

"We know each other. You know that don't you? Sorry. That's rhetorical. You don't have to answer."

The woman cups her hand to the glass to see better or to be seen. She fixes him with a humourless hurry-up smile. He holds up two fingers and mouths, "One sec."

What to say in one sec?

"Do you remember the man you gave the money when we were on Prince Street that first night we got to know each other…"

The woman opens the door, leans in, and says, "I don't have a key. Can I?"

"Okay."

She presses buttons, straightens her hair, frowns at a man's voice saying, "What?"

"It's me. I want…to come back."

"Where were you last night? You made me look like a fool."

"I know what I did. Can I come up? Please?"

The buzzer sounds and she trudges into the building, disappears into a waiting elevator.

Lucien collects himself. "I know about Montréal and I know you can't be with me because it means you'll remember. You'll remember aborting the baby. I want you to remember that I came here and I told you that I love you and I am not angry. I miss you."

He can see his reflection in the glass door. He leans into it.

"What you did is what I would have done if I were you."

He continues, "I'm not asking to start over like we're bankrupts. I don't want a new beginning. If you still love me then we won't forget. We'll love each other despite anything, however painful. Some of it is really, really good."

As he turns to leave, the speaker coughs up the voice of her refrigerator compressor stuttering to life.

A hand knocks tentatively on his door. He rushes to open it, finds Harry on the other side.

"Hi. Is it okay if I visit? I'm in for the refit." Harry lifts the bags he holds in either hand as though in evidence of his arrival.

"You just got in?"

"To town, yes. Can I come in?"

If he could, Lucien would stop himself. The surprise of friendship is too great, too wonderful. Maybe it's exhaustion, the thinning of his defenses against joy.

Harry pushes past and closes the door. "It's nice to be missed. I missed you, too. I'll make coffee. Point to the implements of caffeine."

"You're so much older."

"You're a lot wetter than I remembered."

Over coffee Harry talks about school. He hates it. He talks about sailing. He intends to quit. You can't build a career on vomiting into a bucket. Besides, he'll never meet a better crew. "I'm just down for this and only because you guys are here. I might finish the school year but I won't take another ship."

"What will you do?"

"I don't know what I'm good at, and I don't know what there is. I was hoping you guys could help me." He gets up and goes to the bathroom, comes back with a thick, folded square of toilet paper he offers to Lucien. "Here. You've got snot on your face. Look, it's up to you, but I can hear what's going on if you want to tell me."

"It's nothing. Thermodynamics."

"Sure. You don't have to tell me. Where's Olivia?"

"Home today. Exam she's studying for."

Harry looks at him closely and doesn't inquire further. "I've got to sign ship's articles or I'd stay for supper."

"I didn't offer."

"That's okay. I would have stayed anyway. I didn't realize how much I missed you while I was at my lonely desk at school, banging a calculator against my head. Not enough to cry, but plenty just the same. Do you think anyone's hiring in Halifax?"

"I hope not."

"You're so funny I could almost laugh. Work on that."

"You have grown up."

The night scoops him out. Leaves him empty. He wanders downtown to find the streets a closed shop. From Black Street to Lower Water, a near-rural stillness, quiet, dark buildings, the odd car tailgated by wisps of snow.

Another sleepless night, naked and twisted in a twisted blanket. Someone is knocking. Lucien trips out of bed, kicks off the blanket that grips like a drowning man, gropes his way down the hall, opens to see a well-bundled woman with Olivia's eyes. The woman takes off her scarf and she has Olivia's lips. She removes a glove: Olivia's finger. She puts it to her lips, cutting him off mid- "I didn't expect..."

Olivia tugs her boots off, places them tidily together on the mat, walks past him without speaking. He follows, his mind stupid with words. She feels as she goes, touches the brown plant she gave him, caresses a leaf to pieces in her hands. Touches titles across the bookshelf with her palm, arrives at the still-crooked picture of his parents on the facing wall, where she is stopped. She will correct it, make it straight, he thinks. She doesn't. In the dining room she presses on the table. It's clean, he's cleared it of tarot and takeout and tea. The closed curtains block the dining room window's view of the neighbour's garage. She stares into the paisley-ness of them. She looks at him then, looks him up and down while the words he can't order strangle him. He returns her look, observes that her cheeks are still red from the cold, that she's wearing odd socks the same colour.

"Tell me this," she says. "Why is everyone who visits the past a bad guest?"

"I don't know."

"Me neither."

She drifts into the kitchen, touches a cold element on the stove.

"It's because we're afraid we can't live up to it," he says.

"I think maybe it's because we're time handicapped. We don't know anything about it and it unbalances us and we break things."

"Then we're not bad guests. We're clumsy."

"Break willfully. We break the things that would ruin us. You scared the hell out of me. At the door. My door. You did good. I didn't know how badly I need to win you back. Thank you for clarifying. I've been so...uncertain."

"I have to get clothes."

"You don't."

"I'm naked."

"I see that. Be quiet. Please! Lucien, this is what happened to me in Montréal. This is why what you did today matters."

She takes a deep breath.

"There's a clinic in Montréal on a residential street that Maud knew. She'd been there. We went early. It was a grey day. Cold. And I thought no one would notice, I could just sneak in. I was wrong.

"When we got there, a crowd had already set up on the other side of the street. Christ, what a scene! People with signs with...pictures. Strangers calling me murderer in both official languages." She shakes her head, rubs her arms. "Maud wouldn't listen. The important thing—what mattered most—was for her to get into a fist fight. It was chaos if chaos were a room in hell I was trapped inside with a scream. And Maud's pummelling some guy and some other guy is pummelling her. When in doubt, correct the behaviour of strangers.

"So now I'm alone. Maud is—I don't know—in jail? The room where they put me is that hospital ward shade of green. And I'm thinking, 'This is supposed to put me at ease?' The doctor looks remarkably like Sigmund Freud. You can't make this stuff up.

"No, don't say anything. I have to talk.

"It didn't go well. I got sick. Maud came to see me while I was recovering and I lost it. I'd thought she knew who I was. I was her present. I thought she could advise me—I was her fucking doll! The way she crossed the street. I still see it. Fists of rage. Pounding away at her past. And now I'm thinking, 'Okay, so no one knows me.' And Maud keeps telling me she loves me. That's why she had to throw those punches. I just don't understand. That's what she says. Love. Love. Love.

"No, no, no! Don't say anything. Be quiet. I know what you want to say. You want to try to apologize. For everything. There's no need.

"What you reminded me of today was necessary. I was waiting for you for a month. I was waiting for you to talk like a stranger, to call me the things that they called me in Montréal. To say I murdered us. But you don't seem to be capable of doing that sort of thing. It comes naturally to others but not to you. You love me. It's good love because you're you. I was right. I didn't know you. Now I do."

Her eyes roam the room, fix on his penis as though she's just noticed it. She rocks on her heels.

"Okay," she says. "I know what I have to do. I have to kiss you, and then I have to go away and think."

She grabs him roughly and he's unsure of whether or how to respond. He holds her tight. He can't feel her warmth for the cold of her parka. He holds her tighter until he feels her shape.

"Okay. Okay. This was good. I will call you tonight. We'll talk then. Lucien, I'm going to win you. You're going to let me. I'm…it's…the whole world has taken on the flavour of water. Has that been said before? Romantic language is so crowded. Everyone's been there. I'm going."

He watches her rewrap in her scarf, watches her leave, smiles at her ugly, green parka. Her eyes return a nervous smile. He thinks, 'I'm forgetting something.'

II

So why doesn't she call? He spends the rest of the night in his apartment cooking time. Picking up a pocket novel he'd started and put down during his last leave, *Slit My Throat Gently*, he cannot locate his spot. Nothing about the plot comes to mind. He waits for the phone to rescue him from confusion. It remains silent for five hours. He puts the book down.

Then he drops onto his bed, unable to shut off his mind. In two days, he has not slept.

An hour later, he doesn't bother with the light, showers for work in pitch darkness, back-and-forthing: slumping against the tiled walls, straightening and stepping to the showerhead to wet his hair, slumping back against the wall, lathering, stepping forward to rinse. When he's done, he tracks wetly into the bedroom, picks a towel off the floor, and says, "Fuck." He lies flat on the bed and dries himself indolently like he's fifteen.

He might cab. His mind is wired with exhaustion, his feet heavy and slow. He wants the air, the cool of a still-dark city. He follows his coffee cup down quiet streets.

The ship is red, the gangway steep, no one keeps watch. The rail is ice. A rush of oily heat greets him when he opens the after-house door.

He doesn't know why she didn't call.

Most striking about a return from relief is the physical presence of sound. Always the grunt and sigh, the roar of engines, the steam plant coughing, whirring, so why this silence? New crew will hesitate outside the door at the top of the engine room stairs, prepare themselves before going in. They touch the door, feel the noise, and nod. Lucien has watched them turn to the galley, to their cabins, or the deck, return to where the noise is not and wait for the last possible moment to arrive at the heart of the matter. Not Lucien. His habit is to step into the noise immediately, sometimes with his duffel bag lifted across his shoulder, and allow himself to be absorbed, converted.

Always the voice of the room fills his space, the sounds of machinery turning and pushing. Oscillations. Steam traps clapping and stuttering, steam hammer from a valve opened too quickly, the empty pipework downstream abruptly filled, steam smashing into the nearest elbow with an iron fist, the bull gear whirring at high pitch, the sounds of the crew, yelling to be heard above the din, yelling something necessary at someone unaware.

But not today. He stands at the top of the engine room stairs, struck by the power of the silence. He hadn't felt it before when the plant was cold.

The chief waits below, an unlit pipe in one hand, his glasses in the other, the mist of his breath the only movement.

"Who's there? You. Good."

Lucien fumbles over and they shake hands.

"Not awake yet?" says the chief.

"No."

The cover of the high pressure turbine is unbolted, the winch secured.

"Has it been up yet?" says Lucien.

"No. It's quick work now."

"You don't need me."

The chief shrugs. "You're here. How's the cough?'

"Gone."

"Good."

They take a slow turn through the main deck together. The lighting is indifferent, leaving the furthest reaches dimly lit. The dark spaces feel darker for being voiceless. Some of the machinery is open.

The chief chats pleasantly about decrepitude, every pump, every gauge, every valve in sight commented on as though an irritating neighbour, as though he'll have to build a fence.

At the electrical panel he jiggles a switch.

"Loose," says the chief. "We're bringing on the starboard generator with a loose switch. Good luck synchronizing it. Someday it won't happen. We'll just go black. A new switch has been on order for three months. The company doesn't care. They want to run it into the scrapyard. Just as well they get it over with."

"You expect it to be scrapped."

"Definitely."

The chief's manner is curious. He works the lens of his glasses like a worry stone.

"Is something wrong?" Lucien asks.

The chief turns to a nearby gauge and offers, "It's not something I do. I made a mistake and I want to apologize."

"You don't make mistakes or you don't apologize?"

"Both."

"I'm flattered."

"Stop talking. I could have killed you. I should have known. Do you remember in Sorel when I sent you into the boiler? You could have died of heatstroke. No, no, I know you *didn't*, but you *could have*. I didn't think...clearly. The men are more important than the ship. Anyway, my neighbour died of heatstroke this summer. He worked in a bakery. It was hot. It cooked him. I've been thinking about Sorel since then. And I'm sorry. Don't ever tell anyone we had this conversation."

"I won't."

The chief shakes his head. "It's over for steam. Look at you. How old are you? Twenty-five?"

"Thirty."

"And half your career is as good as extinct. They don't build anything interesting anymore. Everything's gone motor. Self-destruct machines. You fix one piston and you've fixed them all, you've paid your debt to society, but they keep breaking, and it's always the same job. Steam is about logic. It's about prediction. It's like having a child. You have to imagine the problems before they happen. A steam engineer views his day with parental eyes. A diesel engineer waits for the worst. That's when his job really starts. You can have it. When this ship goes, I go."

"Go where?"

"Fishing," says the chief. "Not on the boats. Under a tree by a river with a hook and bobber and a hat. I want a hat."

"Do you want to hear something weird?"

"What?"

"You and I are friends."

The sound of steel-toed boots on the metal stairs belongs to Jon.

"Lucien! How's life?"

"Exhausting. They should make a pill."

Jon shakes with a cold hand and smiles warmly. "I've got some in my dresser."

The chief puts a hand on Lucien's shoulder. "More proof," he says.

"Of what?"

"Proof of the passing of a golden age. In my day sailors didn't do drugs. They drank like men."

"Good one, Pops," says Jon.

More steps on the stairs. The third; breathless like he's lost an argument by running out of accusations. He nods to Lucien, regards the chief's esprit-de-corps grin.

Then they are bent to their task, three of them standing around a five hundred pound cover. The chief presses a switch and the steel cables threaded from the lifting bolts to the metal hook above tighten. The winch rumbles with the strain.

"It's not going to go," says the third.

The chief lays off the button and the wires shrug. He says, "Who's there?"

"Harry." He's at the top of the stairs.

"Where were you?" says the chief.

"No one woke me up."

"Who the fuck did you think was going to do that?" says the third. "We're not standing watches."

"Oh." He exchanges a smile with Lucien.

"Jon," says the chief. "Sledgehammers please."

Jon dodges to the shop, they wait, and the wait is awkward. Were the engines running and communication near impossible, someone would be talking, making conversation with a rush of air in Lucien's face. The silence has silenced them. Harry stares at his feet.

Jon returns, Paul Bunyan-like, four sledgehammers slung over his shoulder.

"Hit on the edge, not the top," says the chief. "For God's sake, don't dent anything. It will mean the ship. We're just shaking the rust and whatever else is sticking it. I pull, you pop. All together on the count of one…two…three…"

The hammers hit the cast steel precisely producing the soft note of a muffled bell, the wires go tight, and the winch heaves with a rattling stutter. The cover does not budge.

"Again," says the chief. "Just a tad harder. One..two…three…"

Four swings stopped on metal make the casing ring a louder soft; while the winch stutters as the wires shiver until the third cries, "Stop, for God's sake," and the chief says, "Yeah." Then: "One more time."

Lucien is impressed by how good the weight of the hammer feels in his hands, which are still vibrating from the impact; imagines the sledge as an extension and reminder of his strength, of his muscular mastery of himself.

The third, says to Jon, "I'll bet you wanted to do this when you were a kid, eh? That bell sound. It's like hitting a church with a sledge hammer."

"Yeah, it's always been a dream of mine. That and being chased by a huge fucking rabbit."

Lucien finds hard, physical work liberating. His mind is freer, more poetic, when he labours.

"Last time, boys. Stay with me. One..two…three…"

The hammers crack, the winch cracks, the shivering wires convulse. A great wind blows as though from a silent trumpet—everyone can see it drop. Lucien does not move. Something compels him to watch.

Harry has taken a step back, aware that something is wrong. He reaches, pushing air at Lucien, and screams, "Go!"

Lucien stands transfixed by the hook's clean passage towards him, not scything but dropping straight as the purest communication. He wants to absorb its beauty.

She wrestles with anger at a coffee shop on University: anger at herself for falling asleep instead of calling, anger at the nine o'clock exam that seems unimportant, anger at the anger of the man and woman behind the counter. She needs a quiet space and, from the violence in their language, the two (employees? owners?) were in a relationship until last night. She can't buy peace. The woman gestures wildly, knocks a coffee pot to the floor. It shatters and Olivia stands up.

"There's a woman."

"A what?"

"A woman."

"Where?"

"By the gangway."

"What kind of woman?"

"I don't know. She wants to see Lucien. I had to stop her from coming up. She's the kind of woman who doesn't like to hear *no*."

The chief stands and pats a line of dust from his coveralls. "Not like this she doesn't want to see him." He shakes his head. Jon and Harry stand on either side. Jon rubs his chin with a bloody hand, leaving a streak of blood on his face.

"Why?" says the watchman, "What's wrong?"

"Someone hit me," says Lucien.

Lucien lies on a blanket on the deck. The skin around his left eye is mottled blue. A streak of blood runs down his cheek.

"I did," says Jon. "And a good thing. You must have been crazy tired. I've never seen anyone fall asleep standing up before."

"He wasn't asleep," says the chief.

"You punched him?" says the watchman.

"Yeah." Jon examines his hand.

"What's the last thing you remember?" asks the chief.

"The last thing…"

"Before Jon hit you."

"I was trying to push him," Jon protests. "I didn't expect to knock him out."

"I'm not sure. It doesn't make sense. I could use a drink," says Lucien.

"I've got a bottle of Lonesome Charlie," says the watchman.

"Who let you on this ship!" cries the chief. "The whole sailing life is going to shit. Harry, go to my office. One of the bottles under the bed isn't empty— brandy, not Kool Aid. Take a glass. Don't fetch the whole bottle."

"What in the blessed name of Jesus Christ is going on?"

It's the captain. He's from Corner Brook and has a low regard for Torontonians, which in the captain's lexicon is anyone not from Newfoundland. But for the slippers on his feet, he's in full No.1. His face is florid with anger.

"Same as I said on the phone." The chief is having none of it. "The winch broke when we tried lifting the casing off the main turbine. Nearly killed Lucien. Had it not been for Jon we would have been mopping Lucien off the deck."

"But everything's okay? You can still lift the cover."

"No point."

"No point? The inspector…"

"Let me put it this way," says the chief. "Lucien's alive but the ship is dead. The casing's cracked. God knows what the damage is to the blades, but it would cost more than the ship is worth in its present condition to replace the turbine— if this fly-by-night outfit, in its present condition, had the money for it. No, the *Douglas* is done. The inspector's down there now if you want it from him."

"What do we do?"

"We fish," says the chief.

Harry is back. "I've got the brandy!"

The captain is staggered. He feels for the bulkhead and leaves mumbling, after which the sound of the engine room is heard, a quick gasp of air at the opening of a door.

"The last thing I remember," says Lucien—he takes the cup from Harry and tosses it back— "is something about a rabbit."

"Lucien? Oh my God, what happened?" Olivia stands on the far side of the compartment. Her pants are spattered with dark spots from water kicked up from running.

"Jon hit me."

"He was going to die," Jon explains, and Harry says. "He was going to get crushed."

The chief clears his throat and takes a step back.

"I fell asleep when I got home. I'm sorry. And then it was too late to call. And then I ran and…my books! I left my books in a coffee shop."

"I don't understand."

"I'm not supposed to be here. I'm so stupid. I left my books on a table."

"What books?"

"I was studying. I ran. Are you afraid?"

"I don't think so."

"Your hands are shaking."

"I was almost killed."

"We'll leave you to talk," says the chief. Jon and Harry follow him into the passageway.

"I'm afraid."

"Of what?" he says.

"Of you getting killed. Of us not remembering. I'm afraid we won't know who we were before everything happened. Our history won't include why we started in the first place. We won't know who we were on the dock, what it was like the first time we held hands. Remember our first kiss—in the airport. How did it *feel*? How can we know? Come with me."

"Where?"

"To get my books."

"No, there's somewhere else. No. Yes. I know. I kept thinking there was something I had to do and now I remember. I had to post a letter. Come with me."

He leads her to his cabin and pulls a letter from the bottom of his closet. "I wrote this before we met that time when the ship stopped in Halifax. Do you remember that night?" She shoots him a look of astonishment. "Sorry. Of course you do. I forgot the letter. It's been here waiting. I don't remember what it says, but I know it's how I felt. I wrote so many letters I didn't send."

"What do you think it says?"

"Whatever it says is the truth."

The envelope is streaked with oil, but the letter inside is clean. It consists of four words written in an engineer's hand like the letters were framed with graph paper: straight-lined *t*, compass-curved *S*, sharp-angled *M*. It reads:

Sun. Moon. Stars. Rain.

ACKNOWLEDGEMENTS

Emily Adams, Jörg Albrecht, Stephanie Bird, Dina Desveaux, Tom Dilworth, Rachel Fitzgerald, Colleen Higgins, Kathy Mac , Michaela Maxey, Chloe Moore, Doug Moulton, Laura Mulroney, Nicole Narbonne, Danielle Price, Vivian Vavassis

"I used to live in the middle of nowhere" was originally published in the chapbook *Astrid Cacophony* (Paisley Cow).

ANDRÉ NARBONNE IS the author of three books and the father of four children. A former marine engineer, he came to Halifax, Nova Scotia—the city in which *Lucien & Olivia* is set—on a crippled tanker in the 1980s and stayed for fourteen years. He has been anthologized in *Best Canadian Stories*, won the Atlantic Writing Competition, the *FreeFall* Short Story Contest, and the David Adams Richards Prize. A short story collection, *Twelve Miles to Midnight* (Black Moss Press), was a finalist for the Danuta Gleed Literary Award. He lives in Windsor, Ontario.